READERS SAY...

I thoroughly enjoyed this book. The characters are well developed and engaging and have plenty of chemistry throughout the pages. The storyline flowed smoothly from start to finish." ~ BookBub Reviewer

"The story and characters grabbed me from the beginning and I couldn't stop reading. I loved the characters and watching them grow together, they were well written and went well together. I found this book amazing with great word building making me feel apart of the story and watching it unfold in front of me. A definite must read for any fan and I can't wait to read more from this author!!!" dornelas122 ~ BookBub Reviewer

"Well, I've read this series completely out of order: 4, 2, 3, then this first one. It worked, but I have to say that I highly recommend reading them in order as the characters continue to feature in the future books. These books have

THE BILLIONAIRE'S MARRIAGE PACT

MELODY ARCHER

WANT TO READ MORE SWEET ROMANCE?

Eliza and Daniel Stevenson's love story is waiting for you to enjoy. Grab your copy of this Free Sweet and Clean Romance!
Go here: https://memorablefictionbooks.com/pages/pb-free-book

To my family. Thank you for your unending belief in me.

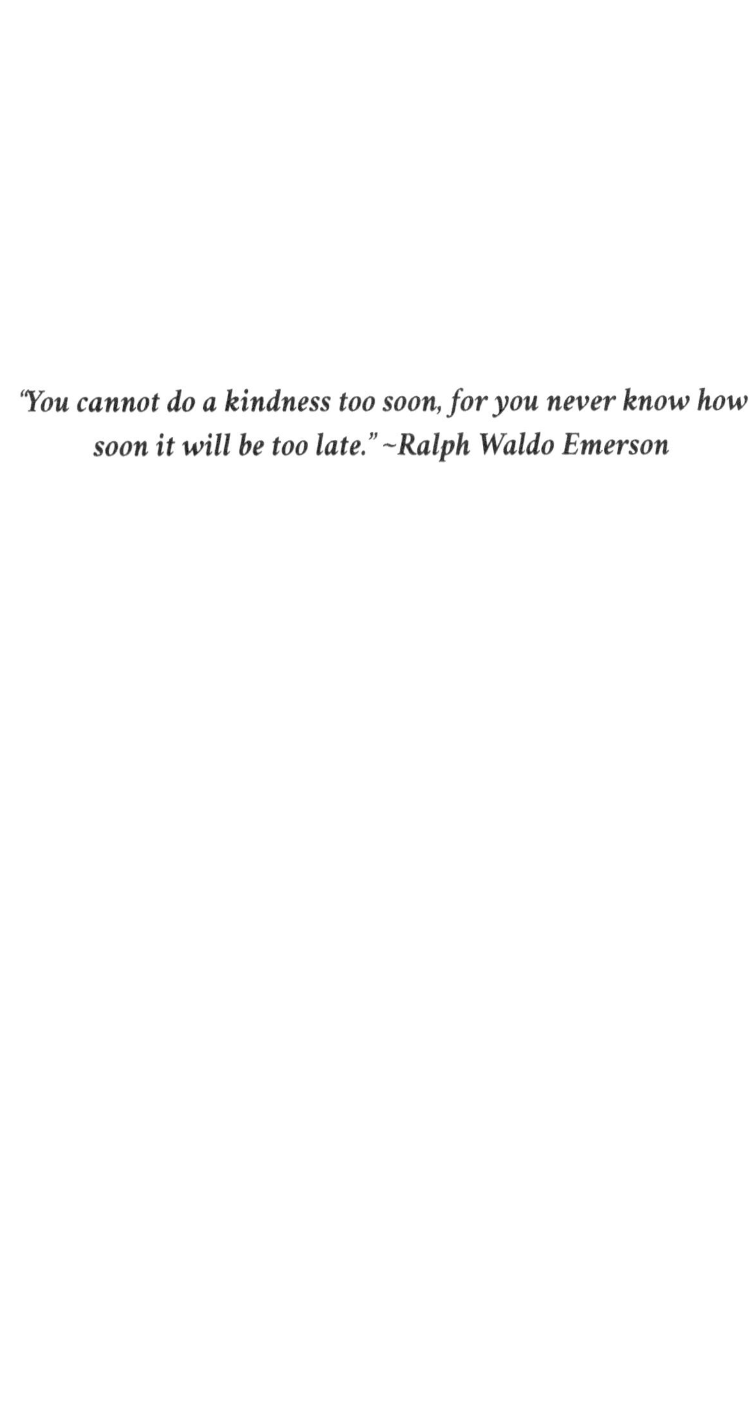
"You cannot do a kindness too soon, for you never know how soon it will be too late." ~Ralph Waldo Emerson

CHAPTER ONE

dam

He needed a wife in less than thirty days.

Adam Daniel Stevenson stared out at the Seattle skyline from his large office on the top floor of Stevenson BeSafe Development Corporation.

The view had always been comforting during the most difficult business negotiations. But, not today.

He closed his eyes, the long nights since the reading of Walker Stevenson's will three days ago catching up with him.

Maybe Great Grandfather wanted control, yet to decide his future from beyond the grave was bullheaded even for him.

The requirement to marry by his twenty-seventh birthday, seemed too much to ask, even for Grand.

Now, he had thirty days to find a wife.

He had dated other women. He'd even been engaged.

But, ever since his heart had been shattered into tiny pieces, he wasn't about to risk another painful heartache again.

In fact, he had made the decision not to marry.

That is… until the reading of Walker Stevenson's will.

Now, it looked like the joke was on him.

Absently, he toyed with his watch, his movements erratic.

He needed some coffee.

That always helped to steady his nerves.

He walked to the nearby kitchenette and poured a cup of coffee.

Walking over to his office desk, he sat on his leather chair. Taking a sip of the hot brew, Adam pondered how he was going to solve this dilemma.

He set his mug down and reached for his old Rubik's cube.

Mechanically, he started twisting the small colored squares. Solutions to problems seemed to come to him as he worked through difficult puzzles and patterns.

As he slipped the last square into place, he felt more clear-headed than he had in days. He set the cube down on his desk and picked up the magazine his younger brother Gabe had handed him yesterday.

On the cover was a picture of him taken by a reporter at a recent charity function focused on helping the city's homeless.

The reporter had added his photo to the front cover of Seattle's business magazine.

He quickly closed the magazine and threw it in his desk drawer. All the extra attention embarrassed him.

Yes, it was true that in the last seven years, Adam and his four brothers had created many security products and development services. Their business had just passed a net worth of eleven billion dollars.

In Adam's mind he was still a normal guy. He was the same guy who was passionate to create software that helped to keep people a little safer from the scammers out there. It was just his small part to play to make the world a better place.

Adam sighed and looked out the window again, his thoughts busy trying to figure out his next step.

Shifting his attention, he grabbed the yellow notepad on the edge of his desk, and set it in front of him. He picked up his pen and twirled it back and forth, the pen dropping every few seconds.

He needed to get his thoughts onto paper to get the clarity he lacked.

Gripping the pen, his fingers shook as he scrawled in black ink the words. *What woman do I know — and trust — would agree to be my fake wife?*

That was a question for which there was no immediate answer.

"I can see the sweat on your forehead from here." Jack stepped quietly into the office.

His brother closed the door, and leaned back against it in his usual cavalier way.

The single scar that ran down his cheek was a gift he had received from one of the leaders of a human trafficking operation after he rescued a girl from their clutches. Adam admired Jack for his daring rescue and for standing up for what he believed in.

"Are you mulling over possible wives from memories of old girlfriends?"

Adam shot a glance at his dark-haired brother and lifted an eyebrow. "I see you managed to get inside my office without alerting Mrs. Appleton."

He put the pen down, leaned back on his chair and grabbed a tissue, wiping the sheen of perspiration from his forehead. He picked up his coffee cup and took another sip, sending his brother a calculated look.

"What?" Jack walked over to the coffee pot and poured a mug of coffee. After tasting the hot brew, he went to sit on one of the comfy leather chairs across from Adam.

He snatched the notepad and read the top line before handing it back. "Hmm, so I was right. You are brainstorming, just like you used to whenever you had to make a serious decision. This time though, you're not pacing."

Adam blew out his cheeks and stood up.

He walked toward the window hoping the incredible view would give him a better perspective on the big step he was about to take.

"Looks like I spoke too soon."

Adam turned to frown at his younger brother who pointedly stared at his shuffling feet back and forth in front of the window.

"It really is annoying how well you know me." Adam rubbed the back of his neck easing some of the tightness in his muscles.

"Okay, all teasing aside. I came early, so I could help you." Jack grabbed the notepad and pen.

"How are you going to do that?" Adam folded his arms across his chest and found himself worrying a little over the mischievous smile that formed around Jack's mouth.

"You are going to brainstorm out loud, and I'm going to write your ideas down. Remember how we helped each other study for those difficult tests during college? This is a little like that, except this time you're in need of a wife, fast."

Adam walked toward Jack, realizing that he needed help. It was true Jack knew him the best out of anyone. They grew up learning each other's strengths as well as weaknesses and helping each other with both. He trusted Jack to help him sort through this new challenge.

Adam sighed pushing back the emotional emptiness that flooded him as he concentrated on qualities he wanted for his wife-in-name-only.

Sighing heavily he said. "All right, let's do this thing."

Adam looked over Jack's shoulder, staring at the notepad and stopped pacing. His heart staggered somewhat under the sudden weight of what he was about to do.

"Writing your ideas down will help figure this out." Jack rested the pen under his chin, watching him.

"I'm not sure about that." Adam paused, adjusting his collar before he went on. "But, I am willing to do whatever it takes. Okay then, let's get this over and done."

Drinking more coffee, he swallowed and began. "As I've been thinking this through, I realized it might be a good idea if I started writing down a list of past women friends and girlfriends. Maybe that will be a good jumping off point."

"Let me have them."

Adam continued. "First off, let's cross Alicia Wentworth off the list. Since I found her cheating on me while we were engaged, she's not someone I can trust."

"Done." Jack wrote down her name and crossed it off. "So, tell me who you are considering."

"As I have been thinking about all the single women I know, I've come up with three possible names." Adam sighed.

"And they are?"

"My high school girlfriend, Betty Johnson. Then there were the two women I dated in college, Lucille Moore and Amelia Thompson." Adam ran a hand through his hair.

Jack scribbled the names onto the paper. "Okay, lets start with Betty. I'm afraid we'll need to scratch her name off the list. Mom said she got engaged a month ago."

Adam sighed. "Okay, that means I have two names left."

"Well, about that. I'm afraid you only have one name." Jack said.

"Why's that?" Adam lifted one eyebrow, wondering how his list of names could have been shortened so quickly.

"Because, when I ran into Lucille's good friend Mia at a coffee shop a few weeks ago, she told me Lucille had decided to become a nun." Jack glanced at him, over the brim of his coffee mug.

Adam closed his eyes and rubbed his forehead. "I can't believe it. Well, I guess I'll need to call Amelia and see if she'll agree to my plan."

"Go ahead." Jack walked to the coffee pot and poured

himself more of the hot brew while Adam dialed Amelia's number.

When he reached her, all he heard was Amelia's voice on a recorded message.

"You've reached Amelia. I have just left for a year long sabbatical in Italy, so I won't be available. However, if this is urgent you can call my parents and they will know how to get in touch with me. Thanks." Amelia's happy voice ended the call.

Adam sighed in frustration. He turned to his brother. "I got Amelia's answering machine. Sounds like she's gone to Italy for a year long sabbatical."

"Hmm. Looks all of your old girlfriends are not available or out of the country." Jack grimaced.

"Yeah. That about sums it up." Adam rubbed the back of his neck. He wondered how he was going to solve this problem. "It doesn't change the fact that I need to find a wife, fast."

Jack looked over at him and asked. "Do you think you'll find a woman who will agree to marry you in less than 30 days?"

"Yes. If she has the right incentive."

"The right incentive. Like what?" Jack glanced up at him.

Adam thought about it for a minute. "Well, I would need for her to agree to a marriage-in-name only for one year. And I want her to agree that there won't be any messy emotions involved."

His brother wrote those ideas down. "Those are unusual requests to ask of your wife."

"*Fake* wife." Adam reminded his brother.

His brother shrugged.

"Also, I'm not sure how you'll be able to control how she feels about you." Jack grimaced.

Adam stopped pacing, turning to his brother in exasperation.

"All right. I'll stop." Jack raised both hands in mock surrender.

Adam nodded and continued walking around the office deep in thought.

He played with his wristwatch as Jack finished writing on the notepad, still finding it difficult to believe that he was actually doing this.

"So, I've got a question." Jack thumped the pen against the notepad. "If you don't want this to be a long-term marriage, how are you going to get this woman to agree to be your wife and stay married to you for the required one year?"

"I'm confident there is one woman out there who will be willing to agree to this marriage as a contract-only sort of arrangement. The million dollars she'll get at the end of the year should influence her decision." Adam didn't doubt that there would be at least one woman willing to marry him for that amount of money.

"Yeah, I guess that makes sense. Likely you'll find a woman who is willing to commit if she is desperate for the money." Jack rubbed his chin and looked at Adam thoughtfully. "Seems like there's not a lot of benefits to this relationship. It's almost like you're marrying a roommate."

"Good, because that's exactly how I want it to be." Adam mentally sorted through all the women he dated and decided that most were either not to be trusted or wanted more from him than he was prepared to give.

"I'm pretty sure mom wouldn't approve of this plan, so that's another reason I need my fake wife to be willing to commit to marriage for one year. I need our mother to believe that this marriage is for real and based on true love."

"That's a good idea, especially with mom longing to hold grand babies on her lap soon." Jack winked at Adam.

"That's a role you can fulfill with your wife, not me. After all it'll be your turn to marry in one year's time." Adam nearly laughed as he saw Jack's face turn a little pale at the reminder. "I see you're starting to have a glimpse of what I'm going through right now."

"Yeah, maybe. But let's get back to finding *your* wife."

Adam couldn't help but smile at how quickly Jack turned the conversation back around.

He had such a short amount of time to find a wife. Would he be able to do it? It would be difficult to find a woman to agree to his terms, but he was determined to see this through.

Adam raked a hand through his hair. He hoped the name of a woman who would be a possible wife-candidate would suddenly spring to mind, but no name surfaced.

Jack stood to his feet and he walked over to the large picture window.

Adam joined him. Turning to Jack, he saw a glint in his brother's eyes.

"I recognize that look. You've had an idea." Adam knew his brother well. "Well, don't keep me in suspense. Let's have it."

A small smile turned up the corner's of Jack's mouth. "I'm not sure you'll like the idea, but I'll tell you anyway."

Adam nodded.

"Do you remember when you used to spend summers at Grand's ranch, working with the horses? You mentioned you'd been getting to know the neighbor girl, Elle Jennings." Jack's dark eyes seemed to glue him to the floor.

"I do remember Elle." Off and on throughout the years, Adam remembered his childhood friend. There were many good memories. But, the memory that haunted him, was the day her father died in the accident.

"Well, I also remember when you said the two of you had become really good friends. In fact, I remember you telling me, that together you had made a pact. Do you remember that?" Jack grinned at the memory.

Adam gave his brother a grudging nod. "I do remember the pact I made with Elle. But, she was only nine years old at the time."

"What exactly was this pact?"

He eyed Jack, and sighed. "It was Elle's idea, but I went along with it."

Adam smiled at the vivid memory of Elle's freckled face grinning up at him. "She said. 'I really like you Adam. You're a good friend. In fact, you're my best friend. I think we should make a pact. I asked her what kind of pact? Elle told me, we should agree that if one of us doesn't marry by the time you are twenty-seven years old, we should marry each other.'"

Jack grinned. "Since you're about to turn twenty-seven, you are close to the age you agreed on. I think you should talk to Elle. Maybe she would agree to marry you. You made a pact after all."

Adam shook his head, annoyed at his brother. "We were children, Jack. That hardly counts."

"Well, I still think you should talk to Elle. You never know. She might agree to this crazy idea. And you're starting to run out of options." His brother's reminder of the deadline, was sobering.

"I'll think about it. But, that's all I'm promising." Adam sighed heavily.

As his brother walked back to grab another cup of coffee, Adam continued to stare out the window.

His thoughts were on Elle.

The last time he saw her, it was at her father's funeral. She had been angry and blamed him for her dad's death. The roads had been icy and when the truck careened into the ditch, her dad died.

Regret still haunted him over what happened.

Maybe she was still angry with him. Would she be willing to talk to him?

Exasperated he got up and started throwing a soft rubber ball against the wall as he continued to think of a solution to his get-a-wife-in-thirty-days dilemma.

Suddenly the sound of the office intercom buzzed, shaking him out of deep thoughts.

"Yes?"

"Your appointments have arrived." Mrs. Appleton's voice reflected that grandmotherly sweetness. After a quick knock on his door, his younger brothers sauntered in with Mrs. Appleton following behind. "I'll just set the food tray on the side table, Mr. Stevenson."

"Thank you Mrs. Appleton." Adam was grateful that the older lady had agreed to be his executive secretary. He made a mental note to raise her salary soon for all the details she took care of for him.

His brothers all found comfortable spots on his large leather sofas. They were in his office today for their quarterly meeting to discuss their latest projects.

For Adam, seeing his brothers all together in one room, gave him an incredible feeling of love and loyalty.

Each of them had gone through the same heartache with the death of their father after his business partner had stolen all the money he had. Their family was left drowning in debt.

They did what was needed to support their mom financially and emotionally. The hardships had been tough to go through, but it also built a stronger bond between them as brothers.

As he looked around the room at each of them, he thought about the differences in their personalities and how that had formed who they were today.

"Jack, why don't you start?" Adam sat on the edge of one of the couches, happy to redirect his focus.

"Well, the in-home security division is going well. In the past year, what seems to be trending upwards is custom built shelters."

Jack rubbed a hand on his chin as he thought more about it. "I'm working with our architectural team right now on some new design ideas that I'm confident will attract even more people who want that extra security for their homes."

"The sales numbers definitely look good, Jack." Luke's

head was bent as usual staring at his laptop computer scrolling through the latest spreadsheet. Adam had always admired Luke's skills for accounting and investing.

"In fact your numbers are close to mine with the launch of the new accounting software." Luke grinned triumphantly.

It was a fact that the software Luke had created specifically to help people keep track of their personal money and business accounts, had been such a success that Luke was now creating a children's edition.

So many parents and grandparents had asked Luke to create something for the younger generation. It was a full package that included tips on budgeting, saving and creating wealth one step at a time.

"Yeah, well don't let it go to your head, because there's sure to be a change coming in my favor next quarter." Jack grinned as he looked around the room at his brothers then pointedly at Luke, rubbing his hands together. "And I can't wait."

"Don't count the rest of us out yet, Jack." Zach the youngest spoke up. "I might be the youngest, but in the past year folks about town and along the west coast have started to notice the boats I've designed and have come to appreciate the high-tech security in them. Motorboats, sailboats as well as yachts. We've had to double our production and I predict we'll double again this next year."

"I have no doubt you will Zach. I'm amazed at what you've already accomplished in a few short years." Adam reached over and fist bumped his youngest brother. "I have a feeling, dad would've been proud of you all."

Zach gave a sideways smile. His cheeks turned red enough to match his auburn colored hair, at Adams words.

There was a subdued hush in the room for a minute as all five brothers remembered their dad who had died when they were in their early teen years.

The doctor had said stress was a major cause of the heart attack as Daniel Stevenson's business partner Simon Black had cleaned out all the bank accounts and created more debt before he disappeared.

The police caught Simon and sent him to jail, but it was an extremely difficult time for their mom and all five sons.

Only a few years later the brothers had formed BeSafe Development Corporation to build security software and systems to help others learn how to be proactive to keep themselves and their businesses safe.

"Gabe, how has it been going with all your personal development projects and speaking events?" Adam turned to look at his blond haired brother, whose bright blue eyes and pearly white smile, gave him the angelic appearance to match his given name Gabriel.

"There's been many more requests from people who want to bring their personal development to the next level, to help them live a better life."

"The speeches and different events seem to be well received. For the next few months, my focus will be on creating more online products and services for easier access." Gabe leaned his elbows on his knees as he looked around the room.

"From what I hear from friends and business connections, they want more of what you're giving them, so that sounds like a solid plan." Adam nodded and then looked at the itemized list on his smartphone.

"Looks like I'm next. So far, the business side of things is going well. The release of my newest software will be ready to go next month and I'm hopeful that this one will do as well or better than the first."

"If it's better than the last one, you've got a winner."

"Thanks, Gabe." Adam stood up and walked over to put his now empty water bottle in the recycle bin.

"I guess that's it. Thanks guys." Adam looked at the itemized list on his smartphone. "Looks like we've covered plans for next quarter so I think we're good. Sorry to cut this meeting short, but I need to get going. I want to get to Great Grandfather's ranch before the sun goes down."

"So, you're going to accept Grand's terms so you can inherit that old homestead?" Zach lifted one eyebrow as he questioned his brother.

"I am." Adam tucked his laptop into its carrying case. "I'm not happy about it, but I want Grand's old homestead too much to miss out on making it mine. And, I've decided it'll take too much time to fight the will in court. So, I will take the weekend or maybe a little longer, for some thinking time."

"You are braver than I am, but I have a little more time before it'll be my turn." Zach's loud sigh of relief seemed to echo off the office walls.

"It'll be your turn before you know it, little brother." Adam playfully clapped each of his brothers on the back, grabbed his jacket from the back of the office chair, and walked out of the office.

He hurried to where his truck was parked and set out to get through Seattle's busy highways.

He was relieved when he finally saw the sign for the small town of Paradise Lake. Adam had spent many summers here growing up and had always appreciated the peaceful idyllic setting.

Adam turned down the long gravel road that led to Grand's ranch. Living on this ranch had always been a dream of his since he was a small boy. A thousand acres sat right next to gentle sloping mountains, connecting to a half mile stretch of lake.

It was the picturesque, perfect life he'd always dreamed of living. Even though he had money to buy any land he wanted, it was this ranch that held his fondest childhood memories.

He belonged here.

Adam parked his truck in front of the sprawling cedar-trimmed ranch house and decided to take a walk along the beach before he did anything else.

Hurrying down the gentle slope that led to the sandy beach and glistening lake water, he heard the loud bark of a dog and the whinny of a horse in the distance. Finally, he reached the end of the path through the trees, and stood on the quiet beach.

Only he wasn't alone.

A large quarter horse stood by the water with a red-haired golden retriever running and barking as it skipped through the water.

"Quiet Ginger."

Adam looked up quickly at the sound of the soft lilting voice.

His mouth curved into a smile at the beauty that stood beside the horse. He walked a little closer and his heartbeat quickened as his gaze swept over her.

The woman's strawberry blonde hair was weaved into a thick braid that hung gracefully over her left shoulder, curling over appealing curves and dipping to her waist where it swayed with every movement.

Long slender legs filled out her faded jeans that were tucked into cowboy boots.

He looked back up, only to be captured by large green eyes, dusted with dark brown lashes and an oval face with freckles sprinkled across her nose and cheeks.

This woman had that girl-next-door look Adam found so appealing.

She was a vision.

Beside her, a red-haired golden retriever's loud bark again broke the silence.

"Hush, Ginger." She turned and leaned over to pat her dog's head. Her lilting voice jolted Adam out of a trance.

She turned to look at him and suddenly recognition dawned on him. For a moment, he was tongue-tied.

"Elle Jennings." He breathed out her name like a prayer.

His blue eyes searched hers.

Adam's breath stilled in his chest, his lungs seized, suddenly paralyzed, as memories washed over him.

He had just been thinking about Elle.

Now here she was.

Once again he was face to face with the daughter of the man whose life he had failed to save.

CHAPTER TWO

lle

"ADAM STEVENSON." Elle whispered the name of the man she thought she'd never see again. "You came back."

Panic pushed her heart against her rib cage at seeing him again after all these years. The horse's reins slipped between Elle's fingers and she grasped them tighter.

An unnatural silence created an invisible barrier between them. Elle forced a pasted-on smile, taking a calming breath before she peered up at him.

He looked the same, yet even more handsome if that was possible.

Bright blue eyes stared at her like two blue pools she could drown in.

A rugged square jawline hinted at the strength and courage her Dad had seen in him. Tiny smile lines were visible at the corners of his eyes, nearly hidden by the blond waves that began near his eyebrows and tipped up by his ears.

Annoyed at her attraction to him, she diverted her gaze back to her horse, rubbing his neck. Tension spread from her neck to her arms as memories came flooding back.

Seeing Adam again reminded her of the girlish crush she'd had on him pretty much the whole time he had worked at her father's ranch.

Three wonderful, terrifying years. Until the accident had destroyed everything including the friendship they'd once had. He'd left right after the truck accident.

Her stomach worked its way into a tight knot, queasy as memories came back from when she was twelve years old.

The rain had come down in waves as they lowered her Dad into the cold, wet dirt, the drops beating down on the mahogany casket like tears from heaven. When she couldn't take anymore, she turned, only to find Adam waiting for her.

Seeing Adam alive when her Dad lay still and cold in the ground, made her suddenly turn on him.

Elle winced a little as she remembered the cruel words that had spewed from her mouth that day. *It's your fault Dad died. You were supposed to be there to help him and to save him, but you failed. Get away from me. I don't want to see you ever again!*

He had just stood there in silent shock before he turned and walked away. Today was the first time in nine years that she'd laid eyes on him.

Elle fiddled with the horse reins as she continued to stare at him. Anger mixed with uncertainty bubbled to the surface.

"You've grown up." His gaze travelled the length of her until he settled to look deeply into her eyes.

"You sound surprised." A faint heat worked its way up to her cheeks. "Why did you come back?"

"Grand passed away and it looks like I've inherited his old homestead." He frowned then looked past her at the lake as if absorbed in deep thoughts. "I'll be taking care of anything that needs to be fixed."

"Sorry, to hear about your great-grandfather's passing. Molly at the town library mentioned it." She stood twirling her fingers through her horse's mane. "So, you're going to be my neighbor." Elle looked at the lake then back at Adam and sighed.

"Yes. And as your neighbor, I'd like to get started on the right foot. We never got a chance to talk when your Dad passed away..."

Elle quickly interrupted.

"I need to get back home." Elle crossed her arms in front of her and looked over to where her father's ranch was hidden by trees. Horses whinnied and dogs barked in the distance and her horse responded back.

The silence was broken.

Sweat formed along her hairline and the world seemed to sway. Seeing Adam again was another reminder of all that she'd lost.

"Wait. Elle, I really want to talk to you. There are some things that need to be said between us." Adam stepped closer. She began to position her foot in the stirrup to get away from his relentless reminders of her painful past.

"I still have a lot of work to get done, and don't really have time to talk." Elle lost her balance and began to sway. Just as she was about to slide to the ground, Adam caught her.

"Are you okay?" Adam leaned over, his strong arms holding her close.

Elle could hear his strong heartbeat, and for a moment, she just wanted to curl up and rest in his strong embrace. His clear blue eyes held a familiarity that she wanted more of. He'd always had that protective streak in him, and today, it was directed at her.

A sudden need for more of his tenderness rushed through her, unsettling her. Pushing away from Adam, she scrambled to her feet.

"Yes. Thank you for your help." Elle forced the words out of her mouth.

"Anytime." Adam looked at her and seemed to come to a decision. A wariness filled her as she waited. "I'll be at your Dad's ranch tomorrow to help with the animals and whatever else needs to be done. Maybe we'll have time to talk then."

"That's not a good idea." Elle worried at the thought of having Adam nearby, but knew she really needed the extra help. She wasn't about to look a gift horse in the mouth. "If you want to help, that's fine, but don't hold your breath that we'll be talking much."

"That's okay. I'll just keep showing up until you do." Adam stepped closer to Elle, so close that she was sure he could see the tiniest freckles on the top of her nose. Warmth spread up her cheeks and she felt flustered.

"Let me help." He whispered in her ear as he put both hands on her waist to lift her up. The touch of his hands left a tingling warmth that wrapped around her belly and made its way upward.

How could she be so aware of his touch after everything that happened?

"Thanks." Elle nodded once, grabbed the reins and urged her horse toward home.

"I'll see you early tomorrow morning." She heard Adam call out but she didn't look back.

THE SUN WAS JUST BEGINNING to rise the next day as Elle walked along the path by the creek.

Her forehead puckered and she rubbed tired eyes from a sleepless night at the thought of seeing Adam again.

The bombshell her stepmother had dropped last night had played into her sleeplessness. The bank had foreclosed on the ranch. They had less than three weeks to pack up and find another place to live.

She had failed her Dad. Tears fell unheeded down her cheeks. This land that her father loved so much, nestled in the mountains just outside Paradise Lake, was going to be lost unless she suddenly found enough money to save it.

Elle swallowed back tears. Her dream was slipping through her fingers.

I'm sorry Dad and Momma. I know this ranch was your dream right when you first got married. It was your little spot on earth that meant freedom and the hope of a fresh start to grow a family together.

When I was little and Momma died, I thought it would be just you and me here forever, Dad. But, then it was only a few short years after you married Lilleth that you left me too. The only thing I have left in the world is this land. But I'm very afraid I don't know how I'm going to be able to keep it.

Her heart plummeted to her toes and the ground seemed to shift under her. *Stupid, naïve, little fool. You should have known better than to believe you could save your Dad's ranch.*

Ginger rubbed against her leg, and Elle knelt down and wrapped her arms around the furry comfort her dog offered. Ginger's soft nose nuzzled her neck and licked the tears from Elle's cheek.

Stopping for a moment, she breathed deeply to settle her emotions.

As she peered up at the mountains, the orange-red skyline signaled the beginning of dawn. She stayed there for a minute longer enjoying the sunrise as it rose above the line of trees by the creek below. It was so peaceful in this place. This was her favorite spot in the world.

But she couldn't stay here long. So many things needed to be done.

"Ginger, come along. It's time to do the chores." Elle patted her dog on the head and stood to her feet.

Her faithful companion led the way down the path toward the barn. Elle hurried to keep up.

As she passed the paddock, vivid memories circled her of Adam helping her saddle her first horse, Beauty. He had always been so helpful and protective.

Elle couldn't stop thinking about Adam Stevenson.

She'd been such a silly girl, following him around like Ginger did, not to mention all the questions she'd asked. Anything, to be close to him.

Now that same childhood crush had grown up from a nerdy eighteen-year old, into an extremely attractive man. She pictured Adam's face with his blue eyes and full lips that swept over pearly white teeth.

Her cheeks heated as she imagined those full lips kissing her own.

Stop it, Elle. This is the same man who witnessed your Dad's accident and didn't save him. Don't you dare think of him like that.

Turmoil flooded her.

Anger rose to the surface. His presence reminded her once more of the death of her Dad and the pain those memories brought to the surface.

Her mother's good friend, Detective Joanna Kingsley had told her they had completed a thorough investigation and found her Dad's death was proven to be an accident.

The roads had been icy, the truck had turned sideways and the oncoming vehicle couldn't stop on those icy roads. Even the Medics who helped him, said that nothing could be done for her father as there was too much internal damage.

Even though reason reminded Elle that her anger was misplaced and she needed to let it go, her heart wanted to have someone to blame – *not someone, Adam.*

Now it seemed they had come full circle. Adam had found his way back to their ranch.

Her stomach clenched like a fist. Why did he have to come back into her life?

From Adam's parting comment, it sounded like he would return to the ranch today. Elle had no idea what to say to him. He wanted to open up old memories, she just wanted to forget.

Glancing across the field she caught sight of the horses in the distance, a rainbow of colors mixed with morning dew glinting off their backs. She admired them for a moment and turned to walk inside the barn. It was time to begin milking their only cow.

Elle rounded the corner by the barn, only to hear whistling coming from the direction of the stalls.

She stopped.

"You came back." She leaned against the door and watched him, admiring how his muscles moved beneath his shirt as he worked. Mentally, she berated herself again for being attracted to him.

She walked over to the horse stalls to check on their feed. Why did she feel like bolting from the barn like a frightened filly whenever Adam was near?

"I don't give up easily." Adam stood and handed her the full pail of milk, his gaze fixed on hers. Elle's hand tingled where his fingers brushed hers. Startled at the electricity between them, she jolted and stepped away from him, the milk sloshing on the ground.

"Thanks." She mumbled and straightened, meeting his gaze. "What do you want, Adam?"

"To help you with the chores."

"Why would you want to do that?" Elle probed, the furrow deepening in her forehead.

"A couple of reasons. One reason is because I really miss working on this ranch." Adam leaned his chin on the hand that clutched the handle of the shovel.

His eyes looked out to the pasture beyond as if remembering. "Ever since I worked for your Dad years ago, a love of working with animals and being outside in the fresh air has stuck with me. Some weird virus you and your Dad infected me with compels me to want to do this again."

Elle couldn't help but laugh at the comparison. "And the other reason?"

"The other reason is that I hope by helping you out you'll eventually talk to me." Adam gave her a sideways smile, which was frustratingly adorable.

"We'll see." Elle's eyes squinted with skepticism. She wasn't about to give in too easily. "You must be a glutton for punishment if you insist on mucking out stalls and working on a ranch on your days off."

She couldn't imagine why he would want to spend his vacation time working on a ranch. But she wasn't about to turn down the offer of free help. She needed it too much.

Adam shrugged and waited.

She sighed, took a deep breath and pointed toward the barn stalls.

"Well, you can start by shoveling out the stalls. I have a few chores I need to get done in the house." Elle tossed a daring look at him, before she picked up the milk and headed toward the house.

He laughed out loud. The husky timbre of his voice created a new row of goose bumps on her arms.

As she went inside the backdoor to the kitchen, she

strained the milk and set it in the cooling pantry. Closing the door to the pantry, she ran a hand over the antique pine cupboards.

This kitchen was her favorite room in this house. She could still smell the warm fresh bread as Momma took it out of the oven.

However, today her thoughts switched back to Adam as she made juice and coffee. She flexed her fingers, still feeling the warmth of his skin on hers.

For a moment, she imagined how it would feel to have his strong arms wrapped around her. Lost in thought, she poured so much orange juice in the cup that it spilled over.

"Elle, what is wrong with you?" Lilleth huffed as she walked into the kitchen. "Why can't you do anything right?"

A cell phone was attached to her stepmother's ear as she grabbed a cup of coffee.

Elle hurried to clean up the spill and sighed at Lilleth's cutting words. "Did you make the muffins and breakfast casserole I asked you to bake for the Bed and Breakfast guests?"

"Yes. It's almost done." Elle poked the muffins with a toothpick checking if they were done, then took them out of the oven. "I'll see that it's put on the side table in the dining room in a minute."

"As soon as you've done that, put some on a plate and bring it upstairs for Carly and me." Her stepmother and stepsister made more work for Elle than their Bed and Breakfast guests.

Elle understood Lilleth was really discouraged by yesterday's news from the bank. It didn't help that her stepmother had just been fired from her job a few weeks ago.

She felt compassion and wanted to have patience with what she was going through. It was difficult to feel kindness toward someone who always belittled you.

Sighing, Elle reached for the dish soap from beneath the sink and turned on the hot water. Many days, she felt more like a maid than a part of the family. Her eyebrows bumped together in a scowl as she battled her way through the melee of dishes.

A sudden knock on the door surprised Elle out of deep thoughts. As she opened the door, her best friend Bella grinned up at her.

"Elle, do you know there's a gorgeous man mucking out the stalls in your barn?" Bella stepped into the kitchen and stood there with her hands on her hips.

"Yes."

"Well, who is he and why is he cleaning out your barn?"

"I'm surprised you didn't recognize him." Elle knew her friend wouldn't leave her alone until she knew all the details.

"That's Adam Stevenson?" Bella walked over to the kitchen stool and sat down and waited for Elle to start talking. "Ah, yes. I heard from Molly at the town Library that Adam Stevenson was back in town."

"I guess he's here to claim his inheritance from Walker Stevenson. I heard Adam will get the ranch, and each of his brothers will each get something else from their great-grandfather that is especially memorable and significant to them."

"Sounds like our small town grapevine has worked quickly as usual." Elle gave her friend a sardonic smile as she washed and rinsed the last dish.

"Yeah, but that doesn't explain why he's here on your Dad's ranch."

"Ah yes. Well, he said he misses working on a ranch and wanted to help. He also wants to talk to me about the accident."

"Adam might be waiting awhile if he wants you to talk about that." Her best friend knew her so well. Elle didn't want to go there, and especially not with the man she still blamed for not saving her Dad's life.

"You're right about that."

"Is that what's got you so worried today? I can tell by the tiny lines on your forehead." Bella traced the smooth line-free skin on her own forehead.

"No, it's because my stepmother told me some terrible news yesterday." Elle stopped washing to look at her friend. "The bank will foreclose on the ranch in three weeks unless we find the money to pay the mortgage."

"Oh Elle, I'm so sorry. That's awful." Bella reached over and squeezed Elle's wet hand. "Well there's got to be a solution. For instance, you could find a man with money to marry."

Elle grimaced. "Not likely. It would be difficult — if not impossible — to find a man to marry that meets my idea of a good husband in less than three weeks."

"I know all about your requirements. Show me what you've written down." Bella held out her hand.

"Show you what?"

"I know you. You've always kept that piece of paper of ideas that are important to you, and that includes what you want for a husband. You've kept that paper tucked inside that book your Dad read to you as a child." Bella stood up and began to walk toward Elle's bedroom. "Your hands are wet. I'll go get it."

Elle quickly dried her hands and followed Bella to her small room that was just beside the kitchen.

Elle had offered to make the small office into her bedroom so that they would have more rooms available for bed and breakfast guests. She never thought her stepmother would take her up on it.

As she walked into her bedroom, she spotted Bella hurriedly searching through the book from her dad.

"Bella, you won't find it. At least, not anymore." Elle sighed, her hands clenched at her side.

"Why not?" Crestfallen, her best friend's smile quickly faded. "Elle, what did you do?"

Elle shrugged and sighed heavily. "I burned it. It was a crumpled up piece of paper filled with old dreams — that I finally realized would never come true — at least not for me."

She collapsed onto the other end of the bed. Lying there, she put her hands behind her head and stared at the ceiling.

Bella coaxed. "Come on, Elle. Even if you got rid of that old piece of paper, all is not lost. You must remember some of the ideas you wrote down."

"I suppose." Elle turned to her friend. Bella's big brown eyes pleaded with her.

"So tell me, please?"

"All right. Not that it will help at all, but I'll tell you what I remember."

A satisfied light came into her best friend's eyes.

Elle sat up, thinking about what she'd written years ago. She was not looking forward to Bella listening to her dead dreams.

That faded piece of paper with all her dreams was something she had written years ago. It seemed so silly now. She'd stopped believing a long time ago that finding a husband was ever going to happen.

"I'll tell you what I wrote down for the man-I-want-to-marry, and then we'll forget about this conversation." Elle began to speak in a quiet, troubled voice. "Here goes."

"*I want a husband who is faithful, kind and who loves me with a forever-kind-of-love.*

Her best friend sighed wistfully. "Yeah, I can see why that would be important to you. You've had to put up with too much unkindness from your stepmother already. It's time you met a man who was kind to you."

"Bella." Elle muttered, irritated by her friend's ongoing commentary.

"All right, I'll stop." Bella sighed and shrugged. "But, I can understand why all those ideas would be important to you. You've always wanted what your parents had — a loving family."

Bella reached for the photo of Elle as a little girl with her parents, lightly tracing their faces with one finger.

Her best friend was silent for a moment, deep in thought. Suddenly, she turned to Elle, a new strength and resolve written all over her face.

"Are you willing to do whatever it takes to save your dad's ranch?" Bella looked her in the eyes — demanding the truth.

Elle swallowed back emotion and nodded.

"Yes. I need to do whatever it takes to save my dad's ranch. I suppose, even if it means marrying a man I don't love." Elle grimaced at the thought.

Her best friend's features brimmed over with unspoken compassion.

Elle rushed to explain. "You know my dream has always been to marry for love. I want the man I love, to love me back. I want the man I love to want to have a family with me someday."

"Well then, who knows? The answer might be right in your own backyard." Bella stood to her feet, facing Elle.

"What are you talking about?"

"I mean, Adam Stevenson. Not only is he inheriting his great-grandfather's ranch, but according to Molly, Adam and his brothers are billionaires." Bella turned, a piercing look in her eyes.

Elle sighed. "Not going to happen."

Bella turned her head, sending her a calculating look.

"I recognize that look. You're hatching some sort of plan." Elle crossed her arms over her chest. "What is it?"

Bella's brown eyes twinkled with merriment. "Do you remember when you told me about that pact you made with Adam? You said you both agreed to marry each other if you were still single when he turned twenty-seven years old."

"I was a child when I made that pact with Adam." Elle huffed. "That doesn't count."

Bella shrugged. "Well, I think you should consider the idea. You have a deadline to save your father's ranch."

Elle stood up and paced the room before finally coming to stand in front of the painting that dominated her small bedroom.

Her mother had painted the portrait of their family, just before she passed away. She looked at the bright glow of her father's green eyes, so similar to her own.

Elle spoke with a quiet, but desperate, firmness. "I might have a deadline to pay-off the mortgage to save my dad's ranch, but I can't see myself marrying Adam Stevenson because of a childhood pact."

CHAPTER THREE

dam

ADAM YAWNED as he carried a hammer and some nails to the fence that surrounded the horse pasture.

Today he wouldn't have minded bringing over one of the workers that he'd hired to repair Walker Stevenson's ranch.

But, the agreement he made with Elle was that he would show up to help her, and he was a man of his word.

He flung a leg over the low wooden fence and stretched.

Last night had been another late night attending a benefit gala. Stevenson BeSafe Developments also helped disadvantaged children.

His brothers, mom and grandparents had all been

there. It had been good to see them, in spite of their attempts at matchmaking.

Last night he had danced with many beautiful women, many of them introduced to him by his mother. Though these women were attractive and accomplished in their own way, something was missing.

When he married - even if she was his fake wife - he wanted a woman who appreciated the simple things in life and who was kind and generous to others.

Someone he could trust.

Of the women he had talked with last night, he didn't think any of them were what he was looking for.

Adam smiled to himself as he remembered his conversation with Jack as they ended the evening.

"So, Adam have you found a lady that catches your interest?" Jack raised an eyebrow as he cornered him at the drink table.

"Honestly, I'm not sure." Adam picked up a drink and grimaced as he looked at Jack. "All the ladies here tonight are beautiful, but they seem a little spoiled and superficial."

He glanced around the room noticing the ladies he'd danced with in their long silk gowns, gold and diamonds glittering in their necklaces, earrings and rings. "I realized tonight, I don't want that. I want a woman who's a little more real."

"Ah, sounds to me like you might be talking about someone you've already met. Am I right?" Jack gulped down the rest of his drink.

"Maybe. I'm just wavering back and forth because marrying someone seems like a big commitment. I mean I'm not looking for love, but it would be good if I could relate to her on a personal level if I'm to stay married to her for a year, right?"

"You have been thinking about this." Jack rubbed a hand over his dark stubble. "So, who are you considering?"

"Elle Jennings."

"So you took my advice." Jack gave a low whistle.

"Elle is as real as they come and she's beautiful. But, she doesn't like me much." Adam looked at his brother for a long moment, still sorting out his thoughts. "It would take a bit of convincing to get her to agree to this."

"You should do it. Ask Elle to marry you. You did make that pact with her, after all. She just might surprise you." Jack pounded his fist gently into his shoulder.

Adam could hardly sleep last night as Jack's words tumbled around in his head.

When he woke up this morning, he made a decision.

Adam would ask Elle to marry him.

He would ask her to be his fake wife. She would get money and he would get a wife and Grand's old ranch.

Now, the hard part would be to convince her to renew their marriage pact and convince her it would benefit them both.

A loud creak at the back door of the house, drew Adam's attention. He looked up and saw Elle walking down the path from the house, her long blond hair pulled back into a ponytail looking freshly scrubbed and beautiful in jeans and a t-shirt.

He was so distracted at watching her walk across the yard, he slammed his thumb with the hammer.

Groaning, he paced back and forth along the fence, shaking his hand out until the pain ebbed into a dull ache.

"Practicing a new dance?"

Adam turned to see Elle leaning against the fence, her arms folded across her chest with a big grin on her face.

"Just a little annoyance. Nothing that won't heal." He stopped pacing, still frowning as he rubbed a finger over his thumb.

"Let me take a look." Elle stood in front of him and picked up his hand, gently rubbing her finger over his thumb. "It's turning black and blue. That must hurt."

Adam nodded, breathing in her lavender scent, the pain suddenly forgotten. Or was it the gentle way she stroked his thumb?

Adam's throat tightened and his heart pummeled against his chest at her gentle touch. Heat ran up and down the length of his arm as her fingers traced his thumb.

Suddenly she leaned down and kissed the tip of his finger. The sweet softness of her soft strawberry colored lips as they touched his thumb made him wish those lips were pressed against his own.

"That's what my Dad used to do when I hurt myself. Then he would ask, 'is it better now?'" Elle gave him a half smile at the memory. A rose-colored stain surfaced on her neck and cheeks and she let go of his hand.

With a throaty chuckle she asked, "So, is it better?"

Adam missed her attention and needed more of it. He stepped closer, and she glanced up at him surprised.

"Not yet." Adam moved closer to Elle and put one hand around her waist while his other hand gently caressed the softness of her cheek. He pulled her closer, drowning in her green gaze.

His gaze shifted downward to her moist full lips. He bent his head slowly, anticipating his first taste of their sweetness.

Without warning, Elle turned her head slightly, and his lips landed on her cheek.

She stepped back, confusion clouding her eyes.

"I can't, Adam." Elle backed away, and with a shaking hand tucked a loose tendril of hair behind her ear. "I have to go. Bella is coming today to help me, and I have to get some things done before she gets here."

Adam watched as she hurried away from him, a little frustrated that she'd put him off.

But, he decided he wasn't giving up in his pursuit of a fake wife.

In fact, to his way of thinking, the chase had just begun.

THE WARM CARESS of Adam's lips lingered.

Elle put a hand to her cheek as she hurried toward the ranch yard. Adam's attempt to kiss her had flustered her, but she found herself wanting him to try again.

Her heart raced and she traced her lips with the tip of her finger. She suspected, next time she would likely give in to her attraction.

Angry for her weakness when it came to Adam, she began hauling things out of the garage with more force than necessary.

It didn't take long before there were tools, tables and

even old sports equipment sitting in the middle of the yard. Before long, Bella drove up the driveway and parked next to the garage.

"Wow, this is a lot of stuff to go through." Bella walked toward her, shaking her head at the large unorganized pile.

Together, they started to sort through Elle's dad's old tools and the sports equipment, and other random things they found in the garage.

They had been sorting for a few minutes, when Detective Joanna Kingsley drove onto the yard in her police cruiser.

Elle had known Joanna ever since she could remember.

She had been her mother's best friend and had always been there for Elle. She'd been sort of like Elle's second mother and fairy godmother all rolled into one.

"Looks like we've got our work cut out for us." Joanna leaned down to give Ginger's head a long scratch.

The front door opened, and her stepmother and Carly walked toward them.

"What do you think you're doing?" Lilleth Jennings charged toward them, waving her hand over the large pile of stuff.

"Sorting through items in the garage, seeing if we can make a little extra money at a garage sale." Her step-mother hovered over them like a threatening storm.

Elle stiffened. She glanced at her friends before lowering her head. Why couldn't her stepmother find something about her she loved?

"As if that's really going to help. What a stupid idea."

Carly scoffed, scrunching up her nose, making her look ten years old instead of seventeen.

A hand squeezed hers and Elle turned to see Joanna stand beside her. Her godmother must have used the detective glare on Carly, because suddenly her stepsister stopped talking and looked away.

"As long as you bring all the money from the sale to me. Not one dime goes to feed those animals of yours, got it?" Lilleth shook a well-manicured finger at Elle.

"Of course." Elle nodded, confused. Since she was fifteen, she'd been responsible for the animals, paying for their upkeep with her own money. The thought of taking anything from her stepmother had never crossed her mind.

"And get this stuff out of the middle of the yard by the time Carly and I come back home."

Elle heaved a sigh of relief as Lilleth and Carly walked toward the car and drove away.

"I don't know what your father was thinking when he married that woman. It drives me around the bend how she talks to you." Joanna hugged Elle. "I can tell you one thing. Your own sweet mama would never have put up with anyone talking to you that way. Or your dad either, I might add."

"Lilleth is extra stressed right now, between losing her job and the foreclosure on the ranch." Elle's shoulders lifted in a shrug.

"No, Elle. Your stepmother has treated you poorly ever since your father died. She's found a way to take everything that's gone wrong in her life and blame it on you."

Joanna held her hand. "It's time that stops. And sweetie, it's time you stop making excuses for her."

Elle shifted from one foot to the other and nodded, unsure of what to say. Making excuses for her stepmother's mean ways had become a way of life. She wasn't sure she knew how to stop.

"Changes aren't easy, but it helps when you have people in your corner who care about you." Joanna squeezed her shoulder, giving a meaningful glance at the big pile of stuff near their feet.

"I know. I appreciate you and any advice you can give me, I really do." Elle put her arm around Joanna's waist, resting her head on her shoulder, needing the comfort that only her second mother could give.

"Hey, you two, slacking on the job?" Bella grinned, crouching in the middle of the pile of equipment.

"All right, we'll get to it." Joanna kissed her on the top of her head and bent down to finish the job.

They were almost done sorting, when Adam walked up.

"Just finished fixing the fence." Adam pulled off his gloves and looked around. "Are you having a sale?"

A warm heat began in her belly that rose quickly to her face. She peered at Adam unsettled and embarrassed by his question.

"We're having a garage sale here at the ranch on Saturday." Elle swallowed to hold back tears that threatened to spill down her cheeks. The thought of selling her dad's things broke her heart.

"Why are you selling so much stuff?" Adam persisted, glancing around. "Your dad's tools, his old golf clubs. Why aren't you keeping these?" He stopped what he was doing, his eyebrow lifted waiting for her answer.

The voice inside Elle's head whispered.

You have to tell him the truth. As embarrassing and humiliating as it is to admit that you've lost the very thing you were desperate to hold onto, the facts are you have to tell him. You've avoided saying anything to him, because of fear. You're scared he'll lose all respect for you or feel sorry for you. You can't control how Adam feels, but you still have to be honest about what's happened.

Sighing she said, "The bank is foreclosing the mortgage on the ranch, and we have to move from here in three weeks. So, the fewer items we have to move, the better."

"Sorry to hear that."

"You didn't know." Elle glanced up as Adam inhaled a deep breath and blew it out slowly. A frown hovered around the corners of his mouth.

His mouth opened suddenly and he closed it just as quickly. It seemed like he wanted to say more, but Elle didn't want to hear his pity.

It wouldn't do any good to hear it. No, she needed to focus on those things that she could control.

"We did it. We're ready for Saturday's sale." Bella looked up. "What else do you need help with?"

Elle glanced around until she spotted the old garden shed behind the house.

"You know what? We should empty everything out of that old shed and see if there's anything in there that can be restored and sold. But first, we should sweep out the garage and put all the stuff we found for the sale back inside. The rest of this broken stuff, needs to be taken to the local recycling center."

"I have a better idea." Joanna interrupted. "Elle, why don't you and Adam go through the shed and decide what you want to sell, and Bella and I will clean and organize this stuff in the garage."

Elle inhaled a sharp breath. That would mean being alone with Adam in a cramped space. That wouldn't work.

"Why don't I help you instead, Joanna?" Elle offered. "Bella, you don't mind helping Adam, do you?"

Bella studied Adam for a moment, a knowing smile turning up the corners of her mouth. She didn't have to be so obvious, Elle thought, her cheeks heating with embarrassment.

Her friend's smile widened. "As much as I would enjoy that, there's a small problem with your idea."

"What's that?" Elle bit out.

"I don't know what you want to get rid of."

Yes, that would be a problem. But the thought of being alone with Adam made her heart hammer in her chest.

"Fine." Elle started toward the shed, motioning once for Adam to follow.

Adam's long legged strides soon caught up to Elle.

"Elle, I want to talk to you about the possible move that you and your stepmother and stepsister are making."

Did they have to talk about this again? This was even more embarrassing than she thought.

"It's not a possible move, it's a real thing that's going to happen. We don't have the money to pay the mortgage, so the bank is taking the ranch." Elle sighed as they reached the garden shed, putting her hand on the metal door handle.

"Wait." Adam covered her hand with his, blue eyes zeroing in on hers, his voice a little unsteady. "What if I told you there was way…"

Suddenly, Adam's words were interrupted by a loud thump.

"There's something moving around in there." Elle slowly opened the shed door.

The sun was still high enough in the sky to shine light inside the darkness of the outbuilding.

"Stay here. Let me go in first. We don't know if it's a wild animal or what." He gently moved Elle behind him and stepped inside.

The shed was cluttered with a whole bunch of gardening tools as well as tarps and other unused items. A musty odor and dust crept up her nose causing her to sneeze.

A soft whimper drew Elle's attention to the corner. Adam stepped forward carefully around the tarps, gardening tools and bags of garden seed.

Elle stood motionless as Adam lifted the corner of the dirty tarp.

A teenage girl sat up, scurrying to the far corner.

Her dark brown eyes grew big. Her teenage body thin and bony as it curled in on itself, like a bruised dog hiding from the world.

Elle crept closer. Adam crouched down so he was eye-level with the young girl.

"Don't be afraid. We won't hurt you. You're safe here." Adam's voice was as soft and velvety as a warm blanket.

The compassion in his voice softened the anger she'd felt toward him. She had always seen him as this cool, somewhat detached computer guy, analytical and distant from the rest of the world.

The teenager covered her upper body with thin arms that poked out from a tattered hoodie.

Her eyes widened and she shook her head from side to side, revealing her disbelief in Adam's words.

Elle put her hand on Adam's shoulder and crouched beside him.

She had a hunch this girl would respond better to a woman. Perhaps she'd been hurt by the men in her life, but whatever the reason, Elle wanted to get through to her.

"What's your name?" At Elle's soft words, the girl relaxed her arms and peered up at Elle. Still, she didn't speak.

"Are you hungry?"

A single nod was all she managed.

"If you come with me, I'll make you a sandwich." Elle stretched out her hand and the teenager put her small one in Elle's.

Adam backed up to let Elle and the girl pass and followed behind.

They walked out into the sunshine and toward the house.

Soon they were sitting at the picnic table outside, with the girl devouring the sandwiches Elle had made.

"What's your name?" Elle hoped the girl felt safe enough with them to answer.

"Bree." She whispered and took the last bite of her sandwich her eyes lowered.

"That's a nice name." Elle whispered. The girl peered up at her, a small smile hovering on her lips.

"Do you remember how you got here?" Joanna's question reminded Elle of her friend's detective instincts.

"Yes." Bree took a deep breath before she began. "I was in Detroit when two men found me. I had run away from my foster parent's home."

The teenager swallowed quickly before continuing. "These men said they were helping me. I noticed other girls in the same house they took me to, had been either homeless, or on drugs too when these men had offered to help. We didn't realize they would feed us and then force us to do disgusting things with their friends."

Bree hung her head for a moment her lip quivering. "They told us we owed them, and we needed to pay off what we owed. In exchange they would feed us and wouldn't hurt us." Bree paused for a moment as tears escaped her big brown eyes.

"It was awful." Bree smothered a sob, before continuing her story.

"But one night at a house party, I managed to escape. I sold my only necklace and used the money to get on a bus that would take me as far away as possible. The gal at the bus ticket counter said the farthest my money would take me was to Paradise Lake. That's how I got here."

"You're here. And you're safe now." Elle let out the breath she'd been holding as Bree shared her tragic story.

A shiver went up her spine at the horrible images that came to mind. She looked over at Adam to see his forehead furrowed, his nostrils flared and his hands clenched into a tight ball.

She reached over, putting her hand over his clenched fist.

He placed his other hand gently on top of her smaller one, keeping them connected in a way Elle hadn't seen coming.

For the first time in years, she didn't feel so alone.

ADAM LOOKED through the large window to view the park across the street from the Stevenson BeSafe Foundation SafeHouse.

The doctors had given Bree the thumbs up to recuperate at the SafeHouse. She needed time and rest to recover from her terrifying ordeal.

Adam made a mental note to thank Jack for having the foresight to hire two mental health doctors who specialized in helping people suffering from trauma.

Elle was in Bree's room now talking with her and helping her get settled.

Elle was never far from his thoughts. Somehow, she had gotten under his skin. He needed to shake off his growing attraction to her.

Adam didn't want to have to deal with the possibility of falling for her. He'd done that once before with an ex-fiancé. It turned out she had only wanted to marry him for his money.

He wasn't about to do that again.

This time it would be a fake marriage, only so they could both get what they wanted.

Elle walked down the stairs and toward him.

"Ready to go?" Adam looked down at her, wanting to run his fingers through the satin-like strawberry blonde hair that hung loose past her shoulders.

Her aqua colored top brought out her green eyes and highlighted her peaches and cream skin tone and rosy lips.

As they walked to the truck, Adam forced himself to stop thinking so much about her kissable lips.

"Is Bree okay now?" He tried to refocus.

"Yes. She's doing better, but she'll need time to heal. I'm glad she's safe now." Elle sighed as Adam helped her into his vehicle. "It's been a busy day. I'll be happy to get back to the ranch."

Adam got in the truck then stopped to look at her. "I thought maybe we could wind down and relax at one of my favorite seaside restaurants, *The Boathouse*." Adam started the truck and waited.

"That sounds nice, but I can't. I'm not dressed for dining out." Elle glanced down at her faded jeans and grimaced.

"I think you look beautiful just how you are now. Besides, you don't need to worry, because I know the owner. And, I am confident he'll find us a table with a good view."

"Well, if you're sure." Elle picked at some lint on her jeans and peered up at him sideways with her brows furrowed.

"I am."

"All right then. I'll need to let my stepmother know I won't be home for supper." Elle pulled her phone out of the pocket of her jeans and sent a quick text.

Soon, they arrived at the restaurant. "This is nice. I sometimes forget what it's like to take a break and just relax for a little while."

It was a good idea.

He only hoped Elle would feel the same way when she heard what he wanted to ask her.

CHAPTER FOUR

lle

ELLE SHIVERED from the warmth of Adam's hand on her back as they followed the waiter to a secluded table.

She sat down and looked around the elegant restaurant. Most of the other women in the diner wore dress pants or dresses.

Fidgeting, she couldn't help but feel a little out of place with her old jeans and scuffed boots.

Elle turned to look out the large picture window overlooking the Seattle skyline.

Her breath caught in her throat.

"It's beautiful." The evening sun shone on the water, lighting the path for the boats on the river below.

The island across the bay was lit up with twinkly lights that shimmered like diamonds.

Children played in the distance.

The scene looked like it had been taken from a Norman Rockwell painting.

She turned back to look at Adam.

"You like?" The corners of Adam's mouth turned up as he stared at her from across the table.

"I do." She smiled in appreciation. "I was just remembering that my Dad and I used to think splurging was going to burger places and small coffee shops. An elegant restaurant like this was visited only in our imagination. So, this is a nice treat."

"You should splurge once in awhile."

"I've needed to save my money for feed and upkeep for the horses, so I could continue with Dad's dream of the horse therapy program for disadvantaged children. We've been lucky to have a neighbor, offer to shoe our horses for free."

Adam's eyebrows knit together as he studied her.

Elle didn't want to bore Adam with details, but she knew that doing something to help make those children's lives a little happier and not so lonely was worth it.

She was glad to see children that had come from trauma situations, begin to heal and let go of fears as they spent time with the horses.

"Penny for your thoughts." Adam's eyes narrowed into a gleam of mischief.

Their waiter poured water in each of their glasses and set menus on the table.

"That might be overcharging." The corners of her mouth quirked up as she looked at Adam.

"Funny, but somehow I don't think so. You always

seem to have a lot of things on your mind and a lot to take care of. It might help to talk it out." He studied her.

"Maybe. I don't know." Elle fiddled with her knife and fork. "I was just thinking of the children who come every week to ride the horses at the ranch. It's been really helpful for them. I see the changes in them from when they started."

Elle paused for a second, swallowing back a torrent of emotion that overcame her when she thought of the kids. "Then I started thinking about our new friend Bree and the heartbreaking stuff she's had to deal with. I guess, a big part of me hopes that by helping these disadvantaged children at a young age, they won't end up in a human trafficking situation when they're older."

Adam's eyes glinted with something that looked a little like admiration.

"You amaze me."

"What do you mean?" Elle frowned.

"You have your own problems to deal with, yet you're still figuring out how to help others." Adam leaned back in his chair, cocking his head to the side as if trying to size her up.

"Just doing what anyone else would do." Elle shrugged.

"That's where you're wrong." Adam relaxed against his chair in thoughtful repose. "Most people who have their own struggles wouldn't bother helping someone else. They would focus on themselves."

"Well, sometimes when we've been through our own hardships in life, it's easier to sense when others are dealing with problems too. It's like our compassion increases for others facing a difficult time." Elle ran one finger around the edge of her glass of water, before looking up at Adam.

"That's true, but you are still an inspiration." His blue eyes flickered with warmth.

Elle bit her lip and glanced away, unsure she was worthy of his appreciation. A wary smile surfaced as she turned to look up at him again.

He placed his hand on top of hers. Then he gently picked up her hand and ran a thumb over each finger one by one.

A warm tingling began in her belly and worked its way up. Heat crept up her face.

The strength in his hands and the work-hardened callouses from helping her at the ranch only drew her to him more.

Elle was grateful when the waiter arrived ready to take their order.

She gently moved her hand away, missing Adam's warmth the moment she did.

They ordered their food and it wasn't long before they were eating, enjoying the delicious seafood dinner.

"I wanted to talk to you about an idea I had about how we can help each other." Adam had just finished his meal, his fingers toying with the edge of his water glass.

"You help me everyday. Which I'm grateful for, by the way." Elle wanted him to know how meaningful his help had been to her. She would be so far behind in her work if Adam hadn't showed up when he did.

"That's not what I meant."

"Okay. How else can we help each other?"

"I'm talking about a way to put a stop to the bank's

foreclosure on your Dad's ranch." Adam's blue gaze studied her.

"You don't need to concern yourself with my problems. You're doing enough." Elle felt really uncomfortable talking about the sordid details of her life.

Heavens, until a week ago, she hadn't seen Adam for nine years.

"I believe we could help each other." Adam took a deep breath, but Elle interrupted.

"How could I help you?" Now her curiosity got the better of her, as she couldn't imagine Adam would need help with anything.

"That's what I'm getting to." Adam explained about his great-grandfather's will and the requirement for him to inherit the ranch.

"So you see, if I don't find a woman I can marry within the next three weeks, I won't get the ranch. And you'll lose your father's ranch to the bank unless you can come up with the money to pay it off, right?"

Elle's face flushed, nodding. She took a sip of water in an attempt to calm her nerves. She didn't like talking about personal details of her life with people.

"If you agree to marry me for one year, I will give you one million dollars. I'll give you half of the money when we marry and the other half at the end of one year. Then we go our separate ways. What do you think?" Adam waited, a confident expectation in his steady gaze.

She choked on the water she'd been drinking. After she got her breath back, she blurted out. "You would give me one million dollars just to be your wife for a year?"

"There would be a few conditions, but yes."

"The money would certainly help save the ranch, but why would you give me one million dollars?" Elle sat motionless, stunned at Adam's marriage proposal. Was he was actually serious about this? And why would he choose her?

"Well that amount of money would pay off what's owing on your father's ranch and you could invest in another property or something to help give you security for the rest of your life."

"True. But why me?" Elle persisted.

"Because lately I was reminded of the pact we made when we were children. You asked me to agree that we would marry each other if both of us were still single when I turned twenty-seven." Adam glanced over at her.

Elle hesitated. "I was a child, when we made that pact."

"Still, I believe right now that pact would really help us both." Adam smiled.

"I don't know." Uncertainty filled her voice.

Adam realized he needed to convince her. "Elle, this makes sense. We can make this work. I trust you. You're my childhood friend. You are someone that I can talk to easily without worrying that things will turn emotionally messy."

He went on hurriedly. "I mean, this needs to be an arrangement where we both know up front that neither of us will fall in love. That's why this would be perfect for both of us. Like a marriage pact of sorts."

"A marriage pact." Elle whispered. She didn't like the idea at all. But she wanted to hear everything he had to say. "You said something about conditions."

"Well yes, I have a few conditions that I would need

you to agree to up front. More than likely, you have conditions too." He hesitated for a moment.

"I'm listening."

"First, we would need to live in great grandfather's ranch house for ninety percent of the time during our first year. Grand's lawyer said this was a requirement to inherit."

"Next, I would ask you to be willing to come with me to certain charity galas and business meetings. And the last request is a little strange, but I can't see any other way to do this."

"My mom and grandparents are romantics at heart. I want both of us to put on a good act to make them think we're in love whenever we see them. That's it." Adam looked at her and asked, "So, does that work for you?"

The first two conditions she could live with, but acting like she was in love?

That would be tough to do. Not because he wasn't attractive, he was. Not because he hadn't been kind to her, he had been.

But because she didn't trust herself to keep the walls up around her heart if she was close to him for an entire year. And she desperately needed to keep the cage around her heart, or she would betray her Dad's memory.

"I'm sure your conditions and this marriage pact is all very reasonable, but it won't work." Elle's back stiffened and she put her napkin on top of her plate.

"I just can't do it. I can't marry you, Adam."

"WHAT DO you mean she said no? Did you explain to Elle that she would get a million dollars by simply agreeing to marry you?" Jack thundered through the speakerphone as Adam paced.

Adam had called his brother, hoping to sort out the thoughts running rampant in his head.

He had just dropped Elle off after a subdued drive home. She had been very polite, only speaking when asked a direct question.

Adam didn't know what to do. He'd been shocked when Elle turned him down, still was, if he was honest with himself.

"Yes. And she told me everything sounded reasonable, but it just wouldn't work for her." Adam paused and continued. "I'm not sure where I went wrong. Did she not like the conditions?"

"Maybe Elle's just scared." Jack offered.

"Scared of me or what?" Adam didn't like the idea of Elle being scared of him.

"I don't know. Maybe she's afraid of being hurt or something." Jack's words held a note of truth to them.

"I'll talk to her tomorrow. I need to find out what's really going on." Adam knew what had to be done.

He needed to understand why Elle refused to be his fake wife.

🐾

ELLE WALKED INTO THE HOUSE, hoping to hurry to her room without being noticed.

"Where have you been? You weren't here to make

supper so I had to do it. I'm way behind now on things I've got to do." Her stepmother's shrill voice carried across the kitchen as soon as Elle walked in the door.

"Sorry that my going out to supper put you behind." Elle didn't think it was fair that she was always the one to make the evening meal.

Sometimes others in the house could help out. "What about Carly? She could have made tonight's meal."

"Carly make supper?" Lilleth smirked. "She doesn't even know how to boil water."

"Maybe it's time she learned. I could teach her how to make a few simple dishes." Elle offered. It would take all the patience in the world to teach Carly to cook.

"Instead of finding excuses, why don't you just show up and do the work you're expected to do!" Her step-mother's eyes narrowed as she stepped closer to Elle. "And just who invited you to supper?"

"Adam Stevenson."

"Adam Stevenson, from the great Walker Stevenson family." Her mocking tones almost caused Elle to lose her control.

But she promised her Dad she'd treat her stepmother with kindness.

"Well, I certainly hope you don't think Adam has any serious interest in the likes of you. You're just the trashy neighbor girl. You're the kind of girl that he'll have some fun with, but won't take home to meet his mother."

"I don't expect anything from him."

"Well, see that you don't." Lilleth's mouth set in a hard line. "And one more thing."

"What?"

"When we move, I don't want you living with us anymore. You're old enough to take care of yourself, and it's time you did." Her stepmother's face contorted into a smug smirk of satisfaction.

A sudden chill flooded Elle's face, traveling the length of her body at Lilleth's words. The echo of her footsteps as she walked away was like the beating of a time clock signaling the end of everything in her life that she loved.

Elle hurried to her small room just off the kitchen, and sat on the edge of her bed hugging her pillow as she digested this new problem.

She needed to talk to someone. Pulling out her cell phone, she dialed Bella's number.

"I have to tell you what happened today." Elle told her about Adam's proposal and her stepmother's decision.

"I'm sorry, Elle. Lilleth is so selfish and mean. I never realized she could be so heartless."

"Yeah, me either. I should've seen this coming." Elle's voice cracked. It wasn't so much being without a home as much as she felt like she was being abandoned once again. "I don't know what to do now."

"Listen to me, Elle." Bella spoke reasonably on the other end. "I think you should really consider saying yes to Adam's proposal."

"But, Bella it's not a real marriage. I wouldn't be marrying the man I love, like I always hoped." Elle sighed, her heart crushing beneath the weight of dying dreams.

"You aren't falling for him, are you?"

"No, I'm not. I would betray my Dad's memory, if I fell for that man." Elle wiped away a stray tear from her cheek, frustrated by the constant mixture of emotions whenever she thought of Adam.

"Elle, you don't know if that's true. Joanna investigated the accident and told you it wasn't his fault." Bella always tried to be the voice of reason in her life.

"She did, but I'm still not convinced." Elle stood up and started pacing.

"From the way he helped Bree, I think he's found his compassion. Maybe he's changed, Elle." It didn't help that her friend pointed out Adam's good qualities. She didn't particularly want to hear about those right now.

"Maybe. But that doesn't change the fact that my Dad is dead and Adam is very much alive." Elle reminded her in a tone that was harsher than expected.

She knew her friend was only trying to help.

"I know, Elle. And I'm desperately sorry about that. You must miss your dad so much." Bella's gentle tone helped calm her emotions. "Listen, this marriage arrangement is not what you've always wanted, but he's offering you enough money to save your father's ranch. That's what you've always wanted."

Bella was the voice of reason in the middle of her storm. "And by the looks of things, in a few short weeks you won't have a place to live anyway."

"I hate it when you're right. All right. I'll talk to Adam tomorrow, but I have conditions of my own." Elle said a new edge in her tone. She was determined to get what she wanted also in this marriage bargain.

"Okay then. Try to get some sleep and I'll call you tomorrow." Bella made kissing noises like they'd done since first grade before she hung up.

Elle put her pajamas on and lay awake for a long time worrying about what to say to Adam before finally falling asleep.

The next morning she was up a little later than usual and by the time she got to the barn, Adam had already finished most of the morning chores.

He was filling the bucket with feed when Elle walked into the barn.

She stood by the door for a minute simply studying him. The muscles in his arms rippled through his thin t-shirt as he hauled down more feed.

He was definitely handsome, there was no question about that. As she watched him, more doubts surfaced. She'd looked up his name online and seen the scores of photos of him with models and other beautiful women.

She didn't have their beauty or their expensive clothes, so why would Adam choose her for his wife, even if it was just pretend? He said he trusted her, and she wouldn't make things messy by falling in love with him.

The problem was there were certain things about Adam she liked a little too much. Some of those details were the fact that he helped Bree and that he loved his mom and grandparents enough to want to please them.

She'd need to constantly remind herself this marriage was only a business arrangement. It was a *fake* marriage.

"Like what you see?" Adam glanced over at her.

Her cheeks heated, and she quickly turned away.

Grabbing an armload from the large pile of clean straw, she walked to the stalls to lay it down.

His low chuckle as she moved from stall to stall sent

shivers up and down her spine. How did he always manage to unsettle her?

She had just finished with the last stall for the horses, when the floorboard squeaked behind her.

"You missed a spot." His warm breath tickled her ear.

Elle stepped away from him, reminding herself she needed to talk to him. He took the rest of the straw and spread it out for her.

Sometimes, he flustered her so much by what he said or did, it made her completely forget what she was doing.

"Elle, why did you feel you needed to say no to my offer?" He took off his gloves and shook out the stray pieces of straw. Staring at her, his blue eyes were compelling and direct.

"Actually, I've changed my mind. I will accept your marriage pact." Elle bit her lip in a nervous gesture. A half-grin turned the corners of his mouth upwards.

"But I have conditions of my own."

"I wouldn't have expected anything less." Adam stood there with his hands in his jean pockets looking relaxed and confident. "Let me have them."

"Okay. First, I want to continue the horse training and therapy that my Dad started. So, I'll need the freedom to go to the ranch to take care of the animals and for the horse therapy sessions I have with the children."

He simply nodded, and Elle continued.

"Next, I want to keep my horses along with my dog, Ginger, and Puss and Boots, my cats. Lastly, since this marriage is just a business arrangement, and we don't want to bring any messy emotions into it, we shouldn't doing a lot of kissing or other stuff." The words rushed out of Elle's mouth before she could stop them.

She had even practiced what to say last night because she needed the courage to get through it.

"The first two conditions are fine, but I might have a little trouble with the last one. Because I do find you very kissable." Adam stepped closer and took both of her hands in his.

Adam went down on one knee, pressing a soft kiss on each of her work-roughened hands. His warm lips on her fingers sent a spiral of tingles up and down her arms.

"Elle Jennings, will you marry me?"

Her cheeks heated as his blue eyes searched her own. She felt their warmth like a physical touch.

"Yes, Adam. I will marry you."

She reminded herself, this was only a short-lived marriage of convenience. What could be a more compelling reason than to save her father's ranch? This is what she needed to do.

Besides, what could possibly go wrong with a marriage pact?

CHAPTER FIVE

dam

ADAM'S HEART jumped in his chest at the sight of Elle walking toward him. Her fingers clung to his grandfather's arm.

His gaze took in her creamy skin, feminine curves, full, and rounded lips.

She was stunning.

Elle moved gracefully between the two rows of wedding guests. He stood waiting, his brother Jack beside him as best man and Elle's friend Bella as maid of honor.

The evening sun shone through the trees surrounding the ranch and each of the wedding guests in it's warm light.

Adam's heart lurched with pride as she looked up at his Granddad a small smile hovering over her lips.

His mom had insisted Elle wear her wedding dress, a traditional gown with soft white satin, that hung elegantly on her. The train spilled its embroidered white waves behind her onto the red carpet where she walked.

A week ago, when Elle casually mentioned they could have the wedding on the ranch, Adam was happy she'd thought of it.

Grand's ranch was the perfect spot.

The history of this place mirrored a blend of old traditions with new beginnings and the love of family mixed with a sense of belonging.

Maybe that was why he loved this old ranch so much.

Just a week ago, Adam had hired the decorator. The countless flowers, the red carpet and the beautiful archway behind him proved that he'd hired someone who did a wonderful job quickly.

He wanted this to look like a real wedding to please his mother and grandparents so he had spared no expense. The caterers had already setup the reception table and the many tables for the guests, ready to serve.

As he looked out toward the small group of wedding guests and saw his mom and grandparents smiling up at him, he had an uncomfortable twinge.

His conscience got the better of him. He might have fudged the truth a little, but he'd never outright lied. He had too much respect for them. But with this fake marriage, wasn't he lying now?

When Adam had taken Elle to meet his mom and grandparents last week, they had been excited to meet her.

They believed Adam and his wife-to-be were in love.

It seemed both of them had played their parts well.

Adam didn't like deceiving them, but he was desperate to do whatever it took to inherit the old homestead.

He had to make this marriage look real.

As he looked down at Elle's beautiful face and form, his attraction to her only grew.

Adam wanted to know all her thoughts. He wanted to know all her secrets. He wanted to know the desires of her heart.

At this moment, he was less worried about acting like he was in love, then about falling wildly in love with her.

He was convinced Elle was no different than Alicia Wentworth, wanting his money more than him. But, the biggest reason that he wouldn't – couldn't let himself — fall in love, was the truth that all the people in his life he cared about, suffered or died. They weren't safe around him. Period.

Only by keeping that reminder in the forefront of his mind, would he keep his heart safe.

Soft music played in the background as Elle finally came to stand beside Adam. Granddad lifted her hand and kissed it, winking at her before he sat down. Elle smiled a little at his mischievousness.

She looked up at Adam who held out his hand. She placed her small hand inside his.

Elle's hand shook slightly, her green eyes large and filled with uncertainty. He squeezed her hand, giving her a reassuring smile as the pastor began to speak.

All too soon, it was time for the vows. Elle's voice was little more than whisper. When it was his turn, he was surprised at the shakiness in his voice as he placed the large diamond on her pale finger.

"You may kiss the bride."

His hands rested on her shoulders.

"You're beautiful." He whispered.

His heart beat wildly at the sight of her upturned face. Large green eyes stared expectantly into his own.

Gently his mouth claimed hers.

She tasted so warm and familiar, as if he had already spent a lifetime with her in his arms. As if she were *meant* to spend a lifetime there.

He had waited for this moment.

Adam tasted her sweetness and cradled her closer in his arms, his lips lingering. The quivering in his stomach changed to a warm heaviness.

He felt strange and hot. He deepened the kiss and the ragged pounding in his heart rose higher and higher until the roar filled his ears.

Heat and something more, something hotter and more potent burst open under his skin, leaving him breathless.

A gentle cough in the background, brought Adam suddenly back to reality.

Forcing himself to step away from Elle, Adam stood perfectly still despite the somersaults circling his stomach.

Gazing down at his new bride, he pushed away the fear that he liked her kisses a little too much. She looked up and Adam imagined himself nibbling on her bottom lip once more.

The need to haul her back into his arms and kiss her again, nearly sent him to the brink of his control.

He sent her a lopsided grin, then smiled at the wedding guests as they were officially introduced as husband and wife.

As family and friends came to offer their congratulations, Adam stood next to his bride feeling uncomfortable with his own emotions.

Pride and happiness that Elle was a Stevenson now were sentiments that were unfamiliar to him, yet felt so right.

"You did good, brother." Jack grabbed him in a quick hug, playfully slapping him on the back.

His brother turned to Elle and kissed her on the cheek before he whispered, "Welcome to the family, little sis. Tell that big brother of mine, he should take a break from working so hard and have a vacation, now that he's married."

"I will." The corners of her mouth turned up as Elle beamed up at him.

"You're in deep trouble now." Jack grinned before walking over to talk with other guests. His other three brothers followed after Jack, each offering their own words of advice now that she was Adam's wife.

Elle smiled at all the attention from his brothers. Adam thought she looked beautiful with her cheeks flushed.

Adam gazed at his bride. How would he manage to keep his heart from falling for his new wife?

Jack was right. He was in deep trouble now.

ELLE PEERED UP AT ADAM, a smile on her face.

She wished she knew what he was thinking. He had definitely played his part today, acting like a man marrying for love.

Heat spread up her neck to her cheeks, the beats of her heart going ninety.

Tiny butterflies that began with Adam's kiss were still tickling her belly.

She'd enjoyed his care and attention a little too much today. That's what worried her.

How would she keep her heart from becoming too deeply involved with her husband? Elle didn't know how she would manage that, but she needed to try.

"My mom's coming this way. She's quite taken with you." Adam whispered in her ear, curling his hand around her waist.

"It's so good to see a young couple in love." Eliza Stevenson slipped her hand inside Elle's and gently squeezed. "Elle, you look beautiful. That dress looks better on you than it did on me thirty years ago."

A sheen of tears shone in his mom's eyes as her fingers caressed the sleeve of the wedding gown.

She dabbed at the stray tears inching their way down her cheeks. "Look at me. I'm a mess. Adam's wedding at the old ranch house and you wearing that dress, well it just reminds me of Adam's father. Today brings back all kinds of wonderful, bittersweet memories."

Her new mother-in-law's words pricked at her conscience.

It was clear, Eliza believed their fake marriage was very real and that her son was in love. Elle would need to be careful not to cause her new mother-in-law any reason to doubt her and Adam's love for each other.

"Thank you for letting me borrow your beautiful

dress, Mrs. Stevenson." Elle was happy Eliza had insisted she wear her old wedding dress.

It was beautiful with its soft satin and simple design that flowed down from her waist in graceful folds. Elle had never worn anything so beautiful.

"Oh, please call me Eliza, or mom would be even better." Eliza winked at her, leaned closer and spoke in a half whisper. "Mrs. Stevenson is my mother-in-law."

"I'd be pleased to call you Mom." Elle's mouth curved into a smile.

She missed this. Elle swallowed back tears that threatened to spill over. It would be a gift to have a mom in her life once more, even for only a short time.

It had been much too long since she had known the gentle touch of a mother. Eliza was kind and compassionate and she looked amazing. When Eliza smiled, tiny crows feet appeared by her eyes. She was beautiful.

"Calling me mom would make me happier than anything. I always wanted a daughter in our family." Eliza hugged Elle.

"I'm glad." Embraced in the warm cocoon of her new mother's arms, she wanted this to last forever. Elle did her best to remind herself that this marriage wasn't real, it was all so Adam could inherit his great-grandfather's homestead and she could save her father's ranch. She needed to remember that.

Out of the corner of her eye, Elle saw Adam's grandparents make their way toward them. Adam's Grandmom wore a teal colored dress that highlighted the green of her eyes.

Adam's Granddad grinned from ear to ear, his wrinkles and grey hair giving him a distinguished look. He had a twinkle in his eyes as he walked up to her.

"So you're the gal who has put that big smile on my grandson's face." William Stevenson walked up to her in a confident take-charge way, a trait that had been passed down to his grandsons, it seemed. He leaned over and kissed her cheek and whispered, "I'm glad."

"Welcome to our family, my dear." Catherine Stevenson pulled Elle into a gentle hug. "Now that you're part of our family, we'll plan a day that's just for us girls. It would be a great way to get to know each other better."

"That would be really fun." Elle easily agreed. Being pampered had never been something she'd had time or money for.

She suddenly realized that for a short while anyway, her life as she knew it had changed.

Soon Adam's mom and grandparents left them to sit down at one of the tables.

As Adam stopped to talk with a friend, Elle spotted Joanna Kingsley.

"I'm glad you came today. It means the world to me." Elle embraced her, needing the support of the one person who had been like a mother to her since she was a little girl.

"I wouldn't have missed your wedding day for anything." Joanna looked at her carefully. "But it happened so fast. Is there anything you want to tell me?"

Elle could always count on Joanna to speak her mind and get right to the point.

"No Joanna, this is not a 'have-to' wedding." She could almost see the wheels turning in Joanna's mind. She knew her well. "Adam and I just realized how much we suited each other."

"Hmm." Joanna eyed her carefully. If she looked too closely, she'd find the cracks in Elle's story. "Being well suited doesn't mean you're in love. Let me offer a word of advice that I wish I'd learned sooner. Don't let any past hurt, pain or fear of love, steal the happiness of your present or future."

Elle swallowed back tears that clogged in her throat and nodded. As usual Joanna had dived deep into the fear that constantly lurked in the back of her mind.

"I'm here for you, my dear. If you ever need anything, you know where to find me, okay?"

"I know, thanks for that. You are the best second mother I could've asked for." Elle smiled at her.

"That part's easy with a wonderful girl like you."

Joanna squeezed her hand and turned at the sound of the music playing in the background.

"I think that's my cue to find a spot to sit at the table. Talk to you later." Joanna squeezed her arm and walked away.

Soon Adam found her and they sat down for the meal. He joined the conversation with his brothers and before long they were passing jokes back and forth to each other.

"I didn't realize Adam had four brothers." Bella leaned over to speak in Elle's ear as the sound of laughter got louder.

"Yes. I didn't realize how close they were to each other."

"Not to mention a good fairy has given them each an extra dose of good looks." Bella spoke softly as her gaze glanced in their direction. "Even with that scar on his cheek, Jack is still very appealing."

"Oh, really?" Elle leaned closer until she was eye to eye with her best friend. "Do tell. What is it about Jack that appeals to you?"

"Stop teasing me. I just think he's handsome, but he's also very irritating and high-handed. He'd be a great husband for some weak-willed girl that doesn't have a mind of her own, but not for me."

"Hmmm. To quote Shakespeare, "Methinks the Lady doth protest too much." Elle winked at her friend.

"Let's not talk about me." Bella's cheeks had turned a lovely shade of red from their conversation, which Elle found very telling. "I'd rather hear about you. How's it going with you and Adam?"

"As well as can be expected. This is just a marriage of convenience, after all." Elle's fingers fiddled with the new wedding ring on her left hand.

"I think it's much more. Adam's eyes are glued to you, Elle. It's like you've just lit up his world. Sort of like the way he's looking at you right now."

Elle turned her head slowly, to see Adam's blue penetrating gaze latched onto her. Her heart beat faster, and the corners of her mouth lifted before she turned to talk to Bella.

"Well, it's all part of the deal we made to act like we're in love when we're with his family. So if you believe it, then our acting skills are better than I thought." Elle shoved back any thoughts of attraction for her new husband.

"Yeah, sure. You keep believing that." Bella gave her a I-don't-believe-you look that she'd used ever since they were in grade school together. "But, just for the record, I think you two would make a great couple if you'd ever get over your hang-ups with each other."

"Well, I'm not convinced."

"Maybe your husband can convince you then, because he's walking this way." Bella spoke in a half whisper, looking over Elle's shoulder.

Elle looked up just in time to find Adam standing in front of her.

"May I have this dance, Mrs. Stevenson?"

"Of course." Elle placed a trembling hand into her husband's steady one.

They walked over to the wooden dance floor that Adam had hired contractors to build. It was a large platform, perfect for an outdoor wedding.

The decorator had added tiny lights to the wood posts that surrounded the dance floor, even the trees around the tables and food area had tiny lights weaving in and out of their branches. The miniature lights gave a fairytale-like atmosphere to the wedding.

Adam's hand on the small of her back was warm as he led her to the center of the dance floor.

A singer crooned a love song in the background, while Adam slid one hand to her waist and held her hand with the other.

Out of the corner of her eye, Elle could see many of the wedding guests watching them as they moved together in this first dance as husband and wife.

"Nervous to see so many people with their eyes on us?"

Adam leaned forward and pressed warm lips against her forehead. "Don't worry, I've got you in case you fall."

"I appreciate that."

She peered up at him. Blue eyes met hers, and an electric jolt rocked Elle, as though she touched a live wire. A breathless panic filled her, and she longed to pull her eyes away, anything to escape this fluttery sensation in the pit of her belly.

"We can do better than this." Adam's warm breath whispered in her ear. Suddenly, he moved both hands around her waist and pulled her closer. Elle put her hands lightly on his shoulders, but Adam moved them higher to encircle his neck.

"Now, we're dancing like newlyweds." Adam looked down at her, the mellow lights shining like a homing beacon in his blue eyes.

The feel of his arms around her brought with it a jumble of emotions. His touch felt warm and gentle, causing her pulse to trip over itself.

When his gaze slid to her lips, desire shot through her, leaving her breathless.

She yearned for him to kiss her right there and then.

Adam tilted her face up to receive his kiss. As his lips met hers, the pressure of his mouth was as light as the evening sun touching the ocean.

As her knees started to weaken from his lingering kiss, Elle forced herself to pull her arms away from around his neck.

"I think we've convinced them." Elle whispered as she stepped back a little.

Their kisses had begun to convince her heart that maybe it would be possible for them to fall in love.

It scared her.

No, that couldn't happen. She needed to guard her heart.

There was no way she could risk loving Adam only to be abandoned again.

WHEN ELLE PULLED her arms away from him, a chill ran up his arms at the sudden loss.

He held his hand gently at her waist and intertwined his other hand with hers.

He loved holding his new wife close.

Her kisses were so sweet, it made him want a never-ending buffet of them.

Maybe, that was the problem. Maybe, that's why she pulled away.

Today was supposed to be a wedding ceremony to help everyone believe they were in love.

He was sure they convinced them, but it also caused another problem.

Suddenly deeper feelings were stirring in him for Elle. Strange sentiments of actually wanting to take care of her and be with her always.

That need scared Adam.

He'd loved before and had suffered heartache.

The simple, yet scary truth was that most of the people he loved suffered pain or died. Including his dad and Elle's dad.

Even though his ex-fiancé had used him, Adam felt guilty that somehow he hadn't been or done enough to make her want to stay.

Adam couldn't be responsible for loving another person, only to see them suffer.

He refused to let that happen to Elle.

That was why he kept a guard up around his heart.

But, around Elle, his resolve crumbled.

It might prove next to impossible not to get closer to Elle, since tomorrow's surprise would put them in close proximity for at least a week.

CHAPTER SIX

Elle

ELLE LOOKED out the window as Adam's private jet circled London's Heathrow airport.

This had only been her second time flying. The first was when she was a little girl, and she'd flown to Hawaii with her mother and father.

The flight had been smooth and incredibly comfortable. She could get used to leather chairs that you could sink into and so much space to move around.

Soon the plane began its descent.

Elle sucked in air and held her breath for a moment.

"You okay?" Adam sat beside her, holding her hand.

"Yes, I just get a little nervous on the landing." She breathed out slowly.

"I can tell." Adam winced, looking down at red marks where her nails had dug into his skin.

"Oh, I'm so sorry. I didn't mean to maim you." Elle rubbed her hand gently on his, hoping to ease the pain.

"Don't worry about it. I'm just glad I was able to help." Adam winked at her and grinned.

Soon the plane taxied to the gate where they would disembark. Elle was glad that Adam had given her time to settle things at the bank before they left Seattle. The title deed to her Dad's ranch was now paid in full.

A big burden had been lifted off of her. Now it was time to fulfill her part of the marriage agreement with Adam. She was determined to make this a fun trip for both of them.

"Before we left this morning, you said where we're going was a surprise, but do I get any more clues?" Elle had always had a difficult time waiting for surprises. Especially when she was certain it was going to be good.

"First, we'll go to our family's penthouse in London. Then I'll take you shopping." Adam stood up and indicated for her to walk ahead of him.

"All right." Elle looked down at her clothes, realizing that the dress slacks and pink blouse she wore were probably outdated. She couldn't remember the last time she'd bought new clothes always preferring the wonderful deals at the thrift store.

But she needed to think of Adam. Most likely, he needed his wife to wear something more in line with the image and brand for his company. She hoped the shopping wouldn't take too long, so they could see the sights here in London.

The two flight attendants stood waiting for them at the door with big smiles on their faces.

"Thank you for taking good care of us today." Elle nodded at them, and the pilot and co-pilot who stood behind them.

"Yes, Jenny and Jane, thank you for the great service as always." Adam nodded at the flight attendants, then looked at the pilots. "Thank you Jim and David for another smooth flight."

"Anytime, Mr. Stevenson."

Elle looked at Adam, and appreciated the warmth of his smile and consideration for people. She wished more people were like that. She noticed these small kindnesses that Adam did, had subtly changed her perspective of him.

As they walked up to the limousine, the chauffeur held the door open for them.

Before long, the limousine had taken them to the underground parking deck of Adam's high-rise.

Stepping out of the private elevator that led to the top floor, Adam keyed in the code and opened the door to his suite.

Elle gasped at the huge windows and high ceilings as she walked into the penthouse. Besides that, everything was white and spacious with a wonderfully large kitchen too.

"This is amazing."

"There's a lot of space, but it feels too stark. Almost like we're in a hospital." Adam ran a hand through his hair.

"Why don't you change it up a little?" Elle walked past the white sofas toward the white walls and massive windows.

"None of us ever has the time. We fly here a few times a year and, then we leave for home again. But if you'd like to hire a decorator to make some changes, my whole family would appreciate it." Adam stood next to her.

"I could do that." Elle looked around the room, but was drawn back to the sun shining through the window. "Oh Adam, what a gorgeous view."

Elle sighed as she could see almost all of the city of London from the high rise.

"I agree."

She turned her head only to see Adam's blue gaze fixed on her.

She flushed.

Elle felt a little awkward today without her usual jeans, t-shirt and ponytail. When Adam said he had a surprise trip in mind this morning, she had just put on her nicest outfit and left her hair down. Today, she was doing all sorts of things that she hardly ever did.

"Your blonde hair has reddish highlights that shine in the sun. I like it when you wear it down." He twirled a thick strand of hair around his fingers.

"Thank you, Adam. I hardly ever wear my hair down. When I'm working it gets in the way." Elle nervously pushed back a stray hand of hair from her face.

"I understand. But this week is about fun, so you don't have to worry about being practical." Adam let go of her hair, and his hand brushed her shoulder like a caress. Tingles of pleasure dotted her arm where he touched her.

"That's true. It'll be nice to have some down time." Elle could feel the air between them charged with the electricity of their attraction for each other.

Her chest constricted afraid of her desire for her new husband. She took a few steps back, quickly changing the subject. "Well as part of the fun, how about if I take you up on your offer to do some shopping?"

"Yes, of course. We'll go to Bond Street, and possibly a few other places. Albert can drive us and drop us off."

It didn't take long until they were back on street level and climbing into the limousine, whisked off to the streets of high fashion.

Elle felt out of her element as Adam led her to stores where the price tags were more than she made in a year.

The store clerk proudly reminded them of what they'd seen on the store window, that their exclusive store was a Royal Warrant Holder where the Queen and the Royal family shopped for their clothes.

The clerk took Elle to the back to try on different dresses and pants and blouses that were of the finest quality and highlighted her slim curves.

With each piece of clothing she tried on, she walked out to the room where Adam waited to get his thoughts on it. With most of the clothes she tried on, he nodded that she should keep them.

After spending two hours, Elle walked out of the dressing room to find Adam handing over his credit card for the largest pile of designer clothes she'd ever seen. The clerks were busy folding and putting the clothes into large bags.

"I don't need everything. One of each would be enough." Elle whispered in Adam's ear, as she stared in shock at the huge pile of clothing and the amounts being added to the bill.

"Elle, let me do this for you, okay?" Adam turned to her, a most persuasive smile hovering on his lips.

"I don't know. It's just so much."

"Well, you'll need to get used to it." Her husband gave her a cocky wink.

"All right. Thank you." Elle realized Adam wanted her to have the nice clothes so she would fit in at the exclusive places he had in mind.

They walked out to the waiting car, and the driver drove them to the penthouse.

As soon as they entered Adam's condo, Elle's curiosity got the better of her.

"Is there someplace special we're going? Another surprise?"

"Do you always want to know my secrets ahead of time?" Adam turned to her and put his hands on his hips, his blue eyes pointed and perceptive.

"I've been known to have trouble waiting for good surprises, yes." Elle curled her lips into a saucy smile.

If his half-grin was any indication, he knew she was going stir crazy, waiting for him to spill the beans.

"Well, I was going to wait until tomorrow, but I might as well tell you now." Adam leaned against the doorframe watching her closely. "We're going to the Royal Ascot horse race. It starts tomorrow, which is why I wanted you to have plenty of choices on what to wear."

As if on cue, a knock sounded at the door. Adam answered it and two people from the store arrived with large bags with her recent purchases. They worked quickly to hang the clothes in the closet of her room.

Just before they left, Adam handed each of them a generous tip.

Elle was overwhelmed and amazed all at the same time with the royal treatment she received today.

"Oh, I'm so excited! I've dreamed of going, but only ever talked about it with my Dad." Elle hurried over to Adam and threw her arms around his waist.

She hugged him and giggled at the thought of finally going to this race. "Thank you, Adam. This is going to be so good."

Suddenly she realized that she clung to Adam's waist. She stepped back and his arms lazily slid off her waist.

Nervously she busied herself with sorting through the clothes that now hung in neat rows in her closet.

"It will be good because I get to spend the day with a beautiful woman, who also happens to like horse racing." Adam grinned and folded across his chest.

"Thanks." A blush rose from her neck to her cheeks. She couldn't believe he thought she was beautiful. She peered up at Adam, her hands fidgeting at her sides.

With her cheeks still heated from his gaze, Elle hurried past him toward the kitchen.

How would she endure a full week or more of Adam's nearness without giving into her desires and kissing him?

ADAM PLACED his hand on the small of Elle's back as they made their way past the set of double doors that lead to the Royal Enclosure of the Royal Ascot horse racing event.

Elle looked beautiful in the short sleeved, off-white

dress designed by Alexander McQueen. Her large white hat and matching shoes as well as the confident way she walked made her look like a princess.

It was all he could do to keep from kissing her. He almost did last night, but Elle had subtly shifted away from him. He didn't know why. He could sense she wanted him too. The sizzling kiss they shared on their wedding day proved it.

Adjusting the collar of his dress shirt and tie under his morning coat, Adam tried to cool himself a little. He told himself it was the sweltering heat that made him feel the need to cool off, but he knew better. Just being near the woman beside him, brought a simmering heat all its own.

He would need to be vigilant about safeguarding his own resolve. His fake wife was affecting him in unexpected ways that had started to break down the walls he carefully built around his heart.

Adam knew his fears weren't only because his ex-fiancé had used and betrayed him.

He was also terrified that history would repeat itself: That someone else he loved would die. That he would fail to protect somebody he loved. That the death of another person he adored and was responsible to protect, would be on his hands.

Today, he needed to make sure that person wasn't his wife.

He was glad they had arrived earlier to see the Queen arrive with Prince Charles and Camilla the Duchess of Cornwall by her side in a carriage pulled by four white horses.

Her Majesty waved to the thousands of people gathered for the opening ceremony, before going to the Royal family's private box.

"Adam, this is so amazing to see the Royal family and to be at the Royal Ascot." Elle swung her head his way, her eyes glowing and her smile radiant.

"I see the horses being lined up to begin the race."

The horses and their jockeys all wore their owners colors as they circled the starting gate. Some horses danced nervously before being coaxed into the starting gate. After a few minutes, they were all lined up.

"Just so you know, the announcer and the organizers of the race won't draw much attention to a horse that isn't part of the Queen's own thoroughbreds. Her Majesty loves her horses." Adam whispered to Elle.

"That's okay. I'll still cheer for my favorite horse."

The slightly nasal sound of the announcer's voice was heard loudly over the loud speaker, announcing the lineup of horses.

"They're ready." Adam grinned at the excitement in Elle's voice. It had been the right decision to bring her to this horse race. He'd never known anyone as crazy about horses as Elle Jennings.

"And they're off." The announcer began to give the audience a play-by-play of the action on the track.

"Number three with the blue colors is in the lead. That looks like a horse that has strength and endurance." Adam whispered to Elle whose eyes were glued to the race.

"Yes. That horse's name is *Nightshade*." Elle looked down at her pamphlet where all the horses were listed along with their jockeys and owners. "But, that's not the horse I'm cheering for."

"Which horse are you hoping will win?" Adam bumped his shoulder against Elle's to gain her attention.

"I'm cheering for the horse with the red colors, he's number five." Elle looked up to see the horses as they rounded the corner and sighed. "It's the horse that's in last place."

"Why would you cheer for a horse that's so far behind?"

"I'm a sucker for an underdog, and I also have a gut feeling about this horse. His name is *Justice*." Elle's wide grin and the sparkle in her eyes made him feel like there was some secret he was missing out on.

"Well, he has now passed two other horses who were falling behind." Adam was surprised that her gut instincts seemed to be on track.

They watched the horses round the final bend on the racetrack and head toward the finish line.

Soon *Justice* had passed all the other horses, with only one other in the lead. It looked like it would be a match race between the *Justice* and *Nightshade*.

"Faster, Justice, faster." Elle whispered her cheer for the horse, her knuckles turning white on the clutch purse in her hands.

It was only in the last fifty feet that *Justice* managed to pull into the lead.

"Justice has certainly surprised us." The announcer's English accent was monotone. "From underdog to winner. He first started racing six months ago. This is Justice's first win, and a big victory for this horse and its owners."

Elle clapped her hands at the win of her favorite horse

and turned to Adam with a big grin. He wanted to kiss her, but knew that needed to wait.

"Let's go sit down at the restaurant and get something to eat. I already reserved us a table for luncheon." Adam held her hand as they walked to the elevator that took them to the fine dining restaurant.

The waiter led them to a corner table that overlooked the lush greenery of the course.

After they had given their order to the waiter, they glanced around.

"This is incredible." Elle looked at the bright lights and flowers that dotted the room and the tables. "I've never been in a restaurant as fine as this. I'll need to store all of what I've experienced today in my memory file."

"What is a memory file?"

"It's where I keep all my very special memories in my life. I write it down in a book and include pictures if I have them, and then I also commit it to memory. That way I can withdraw a memory whenever I need to." Elle took a sip of her water and looked at him, a small smile hovering over her lips.

"I've never heard of a memory file before. That sounds like a good way to keep track of special memories." Adam wondered what other details his wife remembered.

"It is. And you can pull them out whenever you miss someone or feel like you need encouragement that day."

"What is special about today that you want to remember?" Adam's curiosity got the better of him. He really wanted to know her better.

"Coming to the Royal Ascot Racecourse and seeing the Royal family up close was great. And of course, sharing a meal with you in this fine restaurant is on the top of the list."

He smiled and watched her cheeks turn a deep shade of pink.

"I'm glad to hear that. Anything else?"

"Yes. I really loved seeing Justice. It was a pleasure just to get to see him run. That horse seemed to love running just for the sheer pleasure of it. That's the kind of horse I would love to have as my own." Elle's expression turned dreamy for a minute before she came down to earth. "I know it's wishful thinking, but hey, a girl can dream, right?"

"Of course. And I'm glad you enjoyed that race. I think your favorite horse races again in a few days. We'll need to make sure we're here for that."

"I'd love that."

The waiter brought their food and they enjoyed eating in companionable silence for a few minutes.

"What else have you kept in your memory file, Elle? Do you recall sneaking into Grand's stables?" Adam grinned as her face turned slightly red.

"Yeah. I'm sorry I snuck in, but I couldn't resist riding Big Red." Elle frowned a little remembering.

"You were quite daring as a rider when you were young. I remember telling you the one time that you needed to be more cautious when riding a racing horse. It's too risky. You could be seriously hurt." Adam had wanted to protect her but Elle got angry at him for trying to stop her fun.

"I remember. I yelled at you that day." Elle put her hand on his. "Sorry, for that."

"That's okay. I'm just glad you weren't hurt."

"I wasn't hurt because you were always there to protect me." The corners of Elle's lips turned up as she remembered. "Besides, I wasn't the only one who liked racing those thoroughbreds. If I remember correctly, you were on Cowgirl racing against me on Big Red. I seem to remember I won that one."

Elle's grin of triumph pricked Adam's memory of when she was a young girl.

"And I remember your twelve-year-old self, telling me that if I tried harder next time, I might have a chance at winning." Adam sat back in his chair and wiped his lips and hands with a napkin. "You were a feisty one back then. Not much has changed."

"I'll take that as a compliment."

"You should." A half smile lifted the corners of his mouth. "Those races back then were some of my fondest memories. I think that's why I am passionate to see that old racetrack restored. I also want to ask a restoration architect to restore and bring that sprawling old ranch house back to life."

"Adam, that's a wonderful idea. It might be fun, when the racetrack is restored, to start horse races for Paradise Lake and surrounding communities." Elle spoke softly.

"I remember your Dad telling me that restoring the racetrack back to its original condition of how it was in Grand's day, would bring life back into our small town." Adam smiled fondly at the memory. "Your Dad was such an encouraging mentor and friend. I still miss him."

"Me too." Elle gently wiped away a tear on her cheek and her eyes became shuttered.

"I'm sorry. I didn't mean to make you sad." Adam berated himself for bringing up memories of her father. He should've known that would cause her pain.

"It's okay. Let's talk about something else." Her forced smile proved she wasn't really okay.

Adam nodded, wanting to do what he could to see Elle's eyes light up with happiness again.

CHAPTER SEVEN

dam

ADAM LOOKED OVER AT ELLE, who returned a courteous smile.

That's all she'd given him these last four days – polite nods, polite conversation and polite smiles.

This was the last day of the Royal Ascot horse racing event, and they would be flying home tomorrow. Besides coming to the horse race, they explored Westminster Abbey, the National Art Gallery and Kensington Palace.

It was great to be together, but Adam wished he could somehow break through the barrier that Elle had put up.

He realized now that he shouldn't have brought up the topic of her Dad. After all these years, the heartache of her loss was still too painful.

Adam decided he would need to be careful not to press

her on that topic. Maybe they could go back to being good friends again.

He may not fall in love, but he still missed the friendship they had started to grow together.

"Ready for Justice's last race?" Adam leaned over and whispered in Elle's ear.

"Yes. I'm really looking forward to it. He looks to be in fine form today too." As usual, Elle beamed as her gaze swept through the lineup of horses at the starting gate.

What he wouldn't give for his wife to look at *him* like that.

Maybe the surprise he had for her later on today, would earn him at least a quarter of the smile she gave that horse.

"Looks like we're in for a great horse race for this last race." The announcer's booming voice came over the speaker. "Most horse enthusiasts here today believe this is really a match race between Nightshade and Justice."

The horses bolted out of the starting gate, and it wasn't too long before it was Justice and Nightshade in the lead, racing toward the finish line.

Around the last bend in the race track, Justice worked his way forward and won the race by two full lengths.

"That was amazing. I love that horse. There's just something so special about him." Elle sighed and looked at Adam. "Thank you so much for bringing me here. It's been wonderful."

"You are very welcome." Adam placed his hand on the small of her back as they walked out of the Royal Enclosure. "I have a surprise waiting for you. But we'll need to take a short walk to see it."

Her green eyes widened with a mixture of pleasure and confusion.

"A surprise for me? I can't wait." Elle followed at his side as they walked along the sidewalk toward the rows of buildings a little ways away from the racecourse.

With each step, Adam got a little more nervous. He hoped this surprise would help bring Elle back to her usual happy self.

As the long red building that held the stables came into view, Elle grabbed Adam's hand.

"Do I get to see Justice up close?"

"Yes." They walked towards where the owner was waiting with his groomsman holding the reins of Justice.

"Oh, my goodness. May I?" Elle asked the groomsman if she could touch the horse. With his nod, she ran a hand down his neck patting and talking to him the whole time.

It wasn't long before the race horse got restless and the groomsman walked Justice back to his stall.

When they started walking back to the penthouse, Adam spoke.

"Elle, since your birthday is next week, I thought I'd surprise you early." Adam ran a hand through his hair watching Elle closely.

"That was a great gift to see Justice up close. Thank you."

"No, that wasn't your birthday present. Your gift is that horse. I bought Justice for you."

Elle turned to look at him, her eyes as wide as he'd ever seen them.

"You didn't. You bought him for me?" Tears started

flowing down her cheeks and they didn't stop until the driver opened the car doors for them at the penthouse.

"I did. So, do you like your surprise?" Adam asked as they stepped into the suite.

"Yes! It's wonderful, Adam. But it's too much. I don't think I should accept such an extravagant gift." Elle's lashes were wet, and her green eyes shone brighter.

"Well, I think you should. It's the perfect gift for a horse lover like you, Cowgirl." Adam leaned against the door, amazed that she would consider refusing that horse.

She flushed at his nickname for her. "It is a perfect gift. Dad told me when I was ten or so that 'someday I'm going to get you a real racehorse that we'll take to races and see win.' He never got a chance to do that."

Elle wiped away more tears. "I'd given up hope on that dream and now you've given me a chance to have it back."

"I'm sorry your Dad never had a chance to get you a racehorse. Maybe he'd be okay with you having this horse now." Adam stepped closer to Elle, his thumb tucked in his belt loops, uncertain of what to say.

Tears always made him feel so helpless.

"Maybe he would." The skin on her forehead puckered, as she thought about it. "Okay, I will accept that beautiful horse, only if I can race him like my Dad would've wanted me to. As sort of a tribute to him."

"I'm glad."

"And Adam?" Elle walked over to him putting her arms around his waist and kissed his cheek. She stepped back quickly, her face flush. "Thank you for the best birthday gift ever."

"You're welcome. Now why don't you change into

something a little more comfortable, and we'll relax a little. I'll order us a light meal." Adam walked over to the kitchen to get a drink of water. He needed some space away from Elle, or most likely he'd kiss her senseless.

"All right."

Adam ordered their food. It didn't take long for their meal to arrive, and they sat together on the couch, eating their deli sandwiches.

Elle had changed into pink sweat pants and a fitted white t-shirt. With her hair hanging down, she had that carefree girl-next-door look that captivated him.

"Do you mind if I ask you something personal?" Elle wiped the crumbs from her mouth with her napkin and set the empty plate down on the coffee table.

"Go ahead."

"I've been wondering why you didn't ask someone else to be your fake wife?" Elle fidgeted with her hands on her lap.

"I mean, my friend Bella showed me some pictures of the beautiful and elegant women you've dated. You could have had someone like that, instead you got me." Elle flushed to the roots of her hair. "Sorry, forget I asked. You don't need to answer that."

"No worries. How about this, I'll answer that question if you'll answer one of mine, all right?" Adam put his arm on the back of the sofa and waited.

"Okay, that's fair." Elle shifted a little, picking at the lint on her sweat pants.

"First of all, Bella's right. I did date a few women." Adam felt a little exposed telling Elle this, but he wanted honesty between them.

He wanted to gain her trust, which meant he needed to share from his heart. "Most of the time when I dated, it was for a charity gala or business dinner. But I didn't feel anything more than friendship with any of them. That is until I met Alicia."

"Alicia?" Elle's gaze fixed on him.

"Yes. Alicia Wentworth. She's a model and the only daughter of a prominent family. My ego told me she was just what I needed. We got engaged. I started to plan out our perfect life together until one day I went to her apartment and found her with another guy. So, I ended it." Adam peered over at his hand on the couch, a frown gathering on his forehead as he remembered.

"I found out later, she only wanted to marry me for my money. That was a little hard to take."

"I'm so sorry you went through that. It sounds like you're better off without someone like that." Elle put her hand over his, squeezing gently. His hand tingled with the warmth of her touch.

"I am. But that was three years ago, and I haven't had a serious relationship since. That is, until we got married." Adam reached for her hand and began toying with the ring on her left hand.

"Oh." Elle bit her lip and glanced away, feeling a little insecure about their relationship.

"Yeah, it's true. But, back to your question. You want to know why I didn't pick any of those other women to be my wife? Because none of them had what you have. Real compassion and honesty that is so hard to find nowadays." Adam spoke sincerely from the heart. He believed those things about Elle.

"That's the nicest thing anyone's ever said to me." Elle let go of his hand and grabbed the pillow beside her, hugging it to her body. She peered up at him. "Thank you."

"I just call it how I see it." Adam grinned and took a sip from his water bottle before he spoke again. "So, now it's your turn."

"Okay, ask away." Elle hugged the pillow even closer to her body and peered up at him. She looked adorable.

"Why did you decide to do this pretend marriage with me, even though it was clear from the beginning this was something you definitely did not want to do?"

"Wow. That's really putting me on the spot. But, that's okay because we agreed." Elle looked down at the white-knuckle grip she had on the pillow.

She loosened her fingers a little and took a deep breath before she answered.

"I don't suppose because I needed the money to pay the mortgage on my father's ranch would be a good enough answer?" For Elle, it was the truth but he already knew that.

"Not on your life." It was disconcerting how Adam watched the play-by-play of emotions on her face. She knew from Joanna, that her every expression revealed what was going on inside her heart.

Elle took a few seconds to really think about her answer.

"Well, quite honestly, in the last year it has been more and more difficult to live in the same house with my stepmother and stepsister." Elle bit her lip before she continued, "I've done my best to be kind and helpful just like my Dad would've wanted, but it's like Lilleth wants more than I have to give. I can't keep up, and I feel like I'm a failure everyday because of it."

Elle sighed heavily, her shoulders drooping in rhythm with the sound. "So one of my answers to your question is that I was grateful to have a way out from all of my stepmother's demands."

"I can see why that would be difficult. It would be hard for anyone to be treated that way." Adam shook his head, his forehead furrowed as if trying to solve a problem.

"I don't mean to complain. Sure, I've worked hard, but I've also been so grateful to keep the horse therapy programs going for the children. I have a lot to be thankful for." Elle toyed with the ends of her long hair.

"I don't see it as complaining. You're just explaining how hard it's been for you. And I appreciate you telling me. It helps me understand you better and what's been going on in your life."

"Thanks for that."

"So, are there any other reasons why you decided to say yes to my proposal?" Adam's half smile and the way his eyes crinkled, charmed Elle.

"Yes, there is one other thing. I knew that you would treat me fair and be kind, which is something I haven't had a lot of in the past few years." Elle tucked her hair behind her ears, thinking about how much of herself she had just revealed to Adam.

In that moment, Elle knew she really did believe Adam would be kind to her and treat her with fairness.

She thought of how he had helped her on the ranch and how he had treated her with respect on their wedding day. Later, he'd outdone himself when he'd taken her to the Royal Ascot racecourse and bought Justice for her birthday.

He really had gone above and beyond in all that he had done for her.

Doubt started to creep in, chipping away at the layers of hurt and anger she held against him for years. The man she saw before her now, would have done whatever he could to help her dad.

Was it possible that Joanna Kingsley was right, and Adam played no part in her father's accident all those years ago?

She frowned as she continued to think it through.

"Hey, are you okay? For a moment there, it looked like you were having some troubling thoughts." Adam pushed hair gently away from her face and she lifted her head.

Tingles of warmth created a new path where his fingers brushed her cheek with feather softness.

Elle found it disturbing how she longed for Adam's touch. This growing awareness she had of him whenever he was nearby was unexpectedly disarming the carefully constructed barriers she'd placed around her heart.

She reminded herself yet again that they'd both agreed this marriage wasn't real. They both agreed to part amicably after one year. They both agreed that they wouldn't fall for each other.

Grabbing the water bottle, she took a sip in an effort to settle her nervousness.

"Yes, I'm okay."

"Good. And thanks for being honest with me." A corner of his mouth lifted.

"Sure."

She had been honest, except for telling him that everyday she was finding it harder and harder to control her wayward heart.

Maybe what she needed was a good night's sleep. As if in response to that thought, she yawned.

"I'm going to turn in and get some rest for our busy day tomorrow." Elle stood, picking up her water bottle. As she turned to go to the kitchen, she bumped into Adam.

He grabbed her shoulders to steady her. Elle gripped his elbows so she wouldn't fall.

"Sorry, I wasn't watching…" She looked up at Adam, only to see his gaze searching hers before moving downward to her lips.

She stood there motionless and unsteady, captivated by him. He hesitated slightly before he moved his head down, touching his warm lips to hers.

His mouth paused, pulled away slightly then prodded her lips, lingering as if pulling all the sweetness from the honeycomb. Her knees weakened and she moved her hands around Adam's waist to steady herself.

Prickles of awareness began in her belly, creating an unexplored pathway to her heart. Adam finally dragged his lips away from hers and pulled her into a warm embrace, holding her close for a few minutes.

"Sweet dreams." The warmth of his whisper tickled her ear before he stepped back. Grabbing the water bottles he walked into the kitchen.

Elle walked slowly to her bedroom door. Turning the

handle, she looked behind her once to see Adam watching her, his eyes hooded.

She quickly stepped into her room and closed the door. She let out a long sigh and leaned her head against the hard wood.

Elle's thoughts launched into a tailspin. Round and round they went, like the clip clop of horse hooves on a dirt track, picking up speed with every loop.

She wanted to run away. She wanted to embrace him. She was scared she didn't know what she wanted.

CHAPTER EIGHT

lle

"Bella, I'm becoming more and more attracted to Adam. I'm a little worried." Elle put the bridle on her bay mare, double checking the fit.

It was almost time for the children to arrive for their riding lessons.

It had been three days since they had flown back from London, and Adam had worked late almost every night.

He told her he needed to finish the software he'd designed because customers were waiting for it. Elle had spent her time organizing the arrival of her new horse as well as setting the schedule for the kid's lessons.

After a week of growing closer together, it felt like each of them were running to their separate corners.

"Of what?" Bella held the barn door open for Elle as

she brought the horses into the fenced riding area at the Jennings ranch.

"This wasn't part of our deal. I'm worried my feelings for Adam are going to end in heartache." She placed the saddle on the horses back and began cinching the belt.

"So, he kissed you again, huh?" Bella teased.

A flush crept up Elle's face as her best friend quickly figured out the source of all her angst.

"Yes. But it's not only his kisses that make me nervous." Elle patted her horse's neck as her gaze met Bella's steady one. "It's just that he's treated me so well and has even shared what happened with his ex-fiancé. The truth is I care about him, and that really terrifies me."

Elle's shoulders slumped in misery.

"Listen to me." Bella let the door close and walked toward her and put her hands on her shoulders and looked deep into her eyes. "I understand you're scared. I'm sure if I were in your shoes, I would be panicking right about now. But you've said Adam's been really good to you and you've been more open with each other than ever. I say why not enjoy it?"

"But that wasn't the deal Adam and I made when we got married. It's not supposed to be about attraction, it's just about helping each other get what we want, and then we're supposed to go our separate ways."

"Relationships don't usually do what they're supposed to." Bella grinned. "Also, what if Adam figures out he wants more than just the ranch? What if he realizes what he really wants is you?" Her friend put her hands on her hips, head cocked to the side and stared at her with laser-like focus.

"I'd be very surprised. Besides, if that were true, how come he hasn't talked to me since we got back home?"

"He's been busy, same as you."

"Maybe. To be honest, I'm a little annoyed." The mare beside her shook her head from side to side, stomping the ground with one foot.

"You just need to talk to him, Elle." Bella walked ahead of her and opened the door into the fenced riding area.

"I suppose you're right."

Some of the children were already waiting on the other side of the fence. Elle looked up, happy when she saw Bree standing there with her friend Dani.

Elle had stopped by the Safe House as soon as they got back from London and asked Bree if she'd like to learn to ride and take care of the horses every week. Bree had jumped at the chance and asked if she could bring her new friend.

"Why don't we let the newest group members, go first." The children nodded and Bella opened the gate for Bree to step forward.

"Bree, I'm glad you're here. Today we will focus on letting you and the horse get acquainted. Why don't you pet the horse and let her get to know you?" Elle saw the tight line of her lips and how she clutched her hands in a tight knot behind her.

"It's okay. We'll just go slow. And Misty is as gentle as a lamb." Elle reassured Bree.

Elle ran her hand down Misty's neck and rubbed her nose. "Now you try."

Bree hesitantly followed the movements Elle showed her. "Am I doing this the right way?"

"You're doing great. There isn't any right way, not really. This is simply about you and the horse learning to trust each other."

Misty stood still as Bree rubbed her nose. "It's soft like velvet."

The horse nudged Bree a little.

"That's her way of letting you know she likes your touch and wants more of it." Elle chuckled at the gleam of happiness and confidence in Bree's gaze.

Elle sighed with satisfaction. This was why she loved the horse therapy program.

A fresh passion stirred in Elle, since they found Bree in their shed shivering with fear. Now, the once wild-eyed teenager was learning to trust and day-by-day she was recovering.

What Jacob Jennings had begun years ago had become her dream.

She wanted to do what she could to help troubled children, teenagers and adults who suffered from abuse and trauma, to heal.

By the time the session was done, a small smile appeared on Bree's face.

"It might take me a while to warm up to her, but I'm already looking forward to the next lesson." It was worth it to see a little shine of happiness in Bree's eyes.

"You and the horse are learning together how to overcome your fears and to trust each other. It's okay if it takes a little bit of time." Elle took the reins and walked back to where the other students were waiting.

Elle worked with Dani and the rest of the children

until the afternoon sun began to fade, and the children went home.

Bella and Elle were ready to put the horses to pasture, when Elle spotted her stepmother coming their way.

"Elle, just what do you think you're doing, still giving lessons here?" Her stepmother folded her arms, her mouth set in a hard line.

"We talked about this and agreed I would continue the horse therapy program here even after I married Adam."

"I know, but I've changed my mind." Her stepmother clenched her jaw. "It's too loud, and it disturbs me. I don't like the idea of this therapy program continuing on my ranch."

"Except it's not only your ranch anymore. Did you get the notice from the bank that I paid two hundred thousand on the mortgage last week and that it's now paid in full?" Elle wasn't surprised that her stepmother had changed her mind again.

When she lived at home, Lilleth did that on a regular basis.

"Yes, I did." Her stepmother pouted and grudgingly shrugged. "Oh all right, I suppose you can continue your little horse therapy program here. But I don't like it."

The woman glared at her before turning on her heel and stomping back to the house.

"Wow, she's mad." Bella looked over her shoulder at Elle as they led the horses into the pasture and set them free to roam.

"Yes. Lilleth has never liked the horse therapy programs, even when my Dad did them. She didn't complain too much before because I paid for all the feed.

Any money I had left over, I gave to her. But now she's not seeing any benefit from it so she doesn't want me to continue." Elle rubbed her forehead as she closed the gate to the pasture. "Well, I'm not going to worry about it."

"You have enough on your mind. Maybe it's time to go home, find that handsome husband of yours and talk to him." Bella encouraged.

"I will." Elle hugged her friend and waved as Bella drove away. After double checking that everything was in its place, Elle hurried along the path toward Adam's ranch.

But, all her good intentions were for nothing. Elle waited up until she couldn't keep her eyes open anymore. She fell asleep on the couch.

Sometime in the night she dreamed her husband had placed a feather light kiss on her cheek, but when she woke up in the morning, Adam was gone.

A few hours later, a text message appeared on her phone.

Hi. Hope you slept okay last night. That couch isn't very comfortable.

Yeah, it's okay. Was extra tired so I slept soundly. How about you? Elle texted back. She was glad to hear he had come home last night.

I'm good. Hey, my mother just reminded me of our company's anti-human trafficking benefit gala tonight. I'm sorry, I forgot to mention it sooner. Would it work for you to be ready for the driver to pick you up at 6pm?

Ah, sure. It's formal right? Her fingers shook a little as she texted, uncomfortable at the thought of being in the room with so many people dressed up in formal clothes. She'd be like a fish out of water.

Yes. I look forward to seeing you tonight then.

The text ended.

Elle was glad she'd finally get to see Adam tonight. It was a good thing they had done all that shopping in London, at least now she had something to wear. All she had to do was not make a fool of herself in front of Adam or his family and friends.

The afternoon swept by quickly, and Elle enjoyed a nice bath as she got ready for the gala.

As six o'clock drew near, Elle took one last look in the mirror.

She had decided on an off the shoulder sequin emerald green evening gown. Tiny gold earrings shimmered in the light. Her neck was bare without any jewelry.

Her hair was up in a twist with tiny ringlets swaying on each cheek. A French twist was the only hairstyle she knew how to do besides her usual ponytail.

She slipped on matching lacy evening shoes that completed her outfit.

With one last look in the mirror, she took a deep breath. She was as ready as she'd ever be to make her debut appearance into Adam's world.

"Yes, I will be releasing the beta version of this new software in a couple weeks...." Adam spoke to five business associates who had asked about his new security software.

He was just about to share more details when his gaze was captivated by a woman in an emerald green gown standing by the entrance.

His wife. Adam's heart thumped against his rib cage. Elle was a vision. It was difficult to believe this woman was his.

"Sorry everyone, I'll explain more details later. Right now, I need to go see my wife."

Elle. The crooning of her name as it shifted through his brain was enough to make his limbs feel more powerful and his chest swell.

He hadn't really talked to her since they got back from London. It was his own fault.

On some level, the intimacy that had began with Elle during their week away had brought deep seated fears to the surface.

Adam could admit now that the breakup with Alicia had been coming. He hadn't been completely sold on the relationship and felt guilty for letting her down. And, he still had a constant dread that anyone who loved him, would suffer.

A new awareness surged through him that his fake wife was slipping through the cracks in the walls he had carefully placed around his heart.

Tonight he wanted to do what he could to fix things with Elle.

"You look stunning." He leaned over, kissing her cheek.

Her green eyes widened as she looked up at him.

"Sorry I haven't been around much these past few days." He held his arm out slightly and she slipped her hand into the curve of his arm.

"I understand. You've been busy." Her forced smile and the cool tone in her voice convinced him she didn't understand at all.

"Elle, we'll talk later, okay?"

"Sure."

He led her toward a table near the stage where the rest of his family were gathered. Hopefully, the evening would be shorter than usual so he could have that conversation with his wife.

"Elle, how wonderful that you've joined us." His Mom kissed her cheek as she sat down beside her.

"It's good to be here." Elle smiled, nodding at his grandparents and brothers. Adam could tell she was nervous and lightly squeezed her hand.

Gabe stood and made his way onto the stage. He talked about what they did at Stevenson BeSafe Development corporation and then started to talk about the foundation.

"Please welcome one of the biggest inspirations behind this benefit foundation. My Mom, Eliza Stevenson."

"That's my cue." Eliza Stevenson stood and Adam walked her onto the stage. Adam waited by her side until she seemed settled.

His mom's face was beautiful, but pale. Adam remembered Dad always liked the color blue on Mom because it accented her blue eyes. This was her first time speaking at the foundation they started last year to help bring an end to human trafficking.

Her sons had coaxed her into speaking tonight. When she finally agreed, Adam decided he would not miss this first time his mother shared her story.

His mom's voice wavered a little as she began.

"My five sons started this charity with Stevenson BeSafe Development Corporation to do what they could to add to the lives that are saved from human trafficking." Mom's passion shone through the words she spoke to the businessmen and women gathered in the room.

"Tonight, I wanted to share my story so you understand why we are passionate sponsors." His mom's hand shook as she paused to sip from her bottled water. "All the stories you hear from victims of human trafficking are unique in their own way."

"My story is a little different too. I was forced to quit a safe job with my best friend — so I could work at an unsavory casino and bar in an unsafe neighborhood. It was my stepfather who gave me an ultimatum."

"It was either I obeyed my stepfather, or he wouldn't pay for my mother's medical bills. I was nineteen, but I was still living at home because my mother was sick with cancer. My mother was dying and I just wanted a little more time with her. I was desperate for her to have all the medicine she needed."

"Being coerced by my stepfather to work in that dirty bar was like being in a prison cell, being forced to do things I didn't want to do. That is until the day Daniel Stevenson happened upon that ratty old place."

"He discovered the reason I was there and saved me from a horrible fate. He saved myself and others from that place, even though he knew it would cause big problems for himself. He selflessly put his reputation and safety on the line — and for that I'll always be very thankful."

She took a breath before she continued. "My sons and I miss their father very much, we're passionate just like he was to do what we can to help others who are taken and forced against their will. I like to imagine my beloved husband looking down from heaven with a smile lighting up his face tonight, telling us we've done well. All of us have. Thank you for joining with us in supporting this cause."

Loud clapping began, and those in the room stood to their feet.

Adam looked at each of his brothers and saw the shine of pride in their eyes at their mother's courage in sharing her story. Her words had struck a chord with many people gathered at this gala event.

"She did good." Zach's grin was a mile wide.

"Your mother gives new meaning to the word brave." Their Granddad thumped the intricately carved wooden cane at his side.

"That's so true." Grandmom had taken a tissue out of her purse, to dab at the corner of her eyes.

"I had no idea. Your Mom is so courageous." Elle pulled out a handkerchief and wiped away tears that had made their way down her cheeks.

"Yeah, we're proud of her." Adam took a sip of water and watched his mother slowly make her way back to their table. Many men and women shook her hand and were giving her hugs with tears in their eyes.

"Well?" Mom finally made her way back to their table.

"You're amazing. I hope you know that. Dad would be so proud." Adam put his arm around his mother's shoulders and kissed her cheek. She squeezed his hand. They all sat down at the table.

"Thank you." Mom looked pointedly at each of her

sons, her daughter-in-law and at her parents-in-law who sat around the table. Taking her wine glass, she said, "To family."

"To family." Jack spoke and everyone clinked their glasses, smiles lighting up their faces.

"Thanks. But, enough about me. I want to hear about all of you." Eliza turned to her oldest son. "Adam and Elle, you first. I want to hear how your trip was. Are you enjoying being at the ranch?"

"It was great to see the sights of London. We had fun. It's good to be back on the ranch, but there's a lot of work we want to do there." Adam went on to talk about the places they'd seen and the horse races.

"We'll need to come out to the ranch to see what you're up to." Granddad's mouth twitched, and a slow smile appeared. "I grew up on that old homestead. If it's restoration you want, maybe I can remember how the original place looked years ago."

"That would be really helpful, Granddad." Adam nodded.

"You should come to the ranch after my new racehorse arrives in two weeks. Adam bought him for my birthday. It'll be exciting to see him again, but this time on the ranch." Elle toyed with her napkin, an uncertain smile turning up the corners of her mouth.

"Well, that sounds like a lot of fun." Grandmom nodded to Elle and winked at her grandson.

Elle's eyes flickered with happiness. Adam couldn't help it, he was pleased at the welcome she received from his family.

His only regret was that right now he wasn't on the receiving end of Elle's smiles. There had to be some way to bring back the warmth of her smile.

He was determined to try.

❦

"ADAM, do you mind if I steal your wife for a few minutes?" Eliza Stevenson's eyes sparked with fun as she turned to Adam and Elle. "I want to introduce her to a few of my friends."

"Of course."

Elle walked beside her mother-in-law as they made their way across the room to where a group of older women were talking.

"Betty, Mildred and Susan, I'd like you to meet my new daughter-in-law Elle, Adam's wife."

"Oh, it's nice to meet you." All three women spoke at once.

"Thank you. It's nice to meet you too." Elle immediately relaxed around her mother-in-law's friends as they were very welcoming.

"What projects do you enjoy working on, my dear?" Betty quizzed Elle.

"I enjoy working with those who come to the ranch for horse therapy programs for disadvantaged children as well as teenagers suffering from trauma." Elle went on to describe what sort of horse therapy worked for different problems children faced.

"That's wonderful. It just so happens that I'm on the

board for a foundation that is focused on helping disadvantaged children to find programs that can help set them on a better path for their future." Betty grasped her hand and whispered, "I will be contacting you about what spaces you have available for more children. And of course, we'll talk about sponsorship too."

"That would be great, Betty." It was wonderful to find someone else who was also passionate to help children. The sponsorship would be a big help too, as there were always extra costs involved.

"Now that Betty is done cornering you about her pet project, we can talk about other things." Eliza winked at Elle.

As the women talked about each other's families, Elle's thoughts returned to Betty's offer. Now, it seemed her program would be expanded in size as well as finances.

She was excited to begin.

Soon they were done talking and started to make their way back to their table.

"If you'll excuse me, I need to find the little girls room." Elle whispered to Eliza.

"Of course."

Elle walked into the washroom, which was quiet except for one other woman. She stood by the mirror putting on her lipstick.

Before Elle could take a step forward, the woman turned to Elle and looked her over.

She was tall with a model-like face and figure. Right now, a scowl scrunched up her face, diminishing her beauty.

"You came to this benefit gala with Adam Stevenson."

"Yes. I'm his wife." She was about to introduce herself, but the woman continued talking, almost without taking a breath.

"So, you're the woman Adam married." Her voice sounded flat and confident as she gave Elle the once over. "You're certainly not classically beautiful. Hmm, I wonder what he saw in you? Where are you from?"

"Paradise Lake." It was starting to feel like an interrogation and Elle grew more uncomfortable by the minute.

"That small town? Wow, he must have been desperate." Her head shook from side to side, her dark brown shoulder length hair shaking with each turn. "I know two people from there who couldn't wait to leave. It's nothing but a hillbilly dive."

"Maybe some people feel that way." Elle's back stiffened at the insults. "But, I certainly like it."

"That's no surprise. You don't look like you have any class." The woman's gaze narrowed, like a vulture circling its prey. "Well, you won't last long with Adam. He was made for someone who has more style. It's only a matter of time."

"What did you say your name was?"

She glided past Elle, only to turn as she opened the door.

"Alicia Wentworth."

The door closed with a soft ticking sound, like the sound of a clock that was almost out of time.

Elle tried to ignore the inkling of doubt that licked at the hairs on the back of her neck.

The worst part was, Alicia Wentworth was right.

Elle lacked all those things that Adam needed in a wife. She didn't have the charm, sophistication or beauty that was important to a man like Adam.

She wondered how long it would be, before Adam realized it too.

dam

"UGGH. Your dog got me all wet."

Ginger shook her wet fur for a second time in a row spraying Adam and covering him with water and a little mud. Elle hurried to grab two towels, one for Adam and one for Ginger and her mess.

"Can't you see she's shivering from the rain?" Elle and Adam had just got back to the ranch from the benefit gala.

They had both changed into jeans and t-shirts to get more comfortable, but now it looked like at least one of them would need to change again.

"Yes, but I thought dogs were supposed to be outside. Isn't that why they have all that thick fur?" Adam rubbed the muddy brown spots on his hands and dabbed at those on his shirt.

"Well, when the outside weather gets chilly like this, she gets really cold. And I've sort of spoiled Ginger a little by letting her inside the house when she's cold." Elle shrugged. "I'll clean her up so she won't track dirt and mud everywhere."

Elle carried the very muddy dog to the bathroom for a quick bath, thinking about the horrible way this evening had ended.

She bit her lip, as she remembered Alicia's awful words. Niggling seeds of doubt were planted. This may be a marriage of convenience, but what if Adam settled for second best?

Was that why he married her? Maybe he hadn't told her the whole truth about why he married her when they were at the Royal Ascot horse race.

Doubt and fears rose to the surface from a deep place as she thought about the impossible situation she was in.

Now more than ever, she believed her stepmother and Adam's ex-fiancé was right.

She was the trashy poor girl next door whose unrefined ways would end up being a hindrance to Adam. Even tonight's argument about bringing the dog in the house proved that she didn't belong in his world.

The problem was she didn't know what to do about it.

She finished cleaning her dog and wiped away the last of her tears, determined not to let Adam see her heartache.

Rubbing off the last of the muddy water splats on his face, Adam sighed and went to his bedroom to change.

He hadn't wanted to begin their evening together by being impatient or sharp with Elle.

The truth was, he loved dogs, but was annoyed by the problems he had to deal with in his business.

It was time to make things right with Elle.

Adam walked back to the kitchen, only to find his wife sitting on the floor beside Ginger, pouring food into the dog dish.

"Hey." He crouched beside her and put his hand on her shoulder. A line appeared between her brows as she studied him, hesitation in her green eyes. "I'm sorry, I shouldn't have snapped at you. Forgive me?"

"Sure." Elle got up. Adam took the bag of dog food from his wife and put it back in its place.

Adam stood up and followed her to the pantry. He leaned his shoulder on the doorframe watching Elle. He wasn't convinced all was well.

"I'd like to start the evening over. Again, I am sorry about snapping at you about the dog. This is your house now too and I want you to feel free to bring Ginger inside whenever you please." His brows puckered in concern as he watched her.

Elle stared at him a few moments before she nodded. "I accept your apology and I forgive you. I'm sure we'll both need to be patient with each other as we adjust to being married and living in the same house."

"I agree." A sigh of relief escaped Adam's lips. "Let's pretend all of that unpleasantness was from some disagreeable stranger who has now been banished from the kingdom." Adam gave her a half smile as he fidgeted.

The corners of her mouth quirked up.

"What do you say to that?"

"As long as you promise the gates are locked so that stranger can't get back in." Even though her gaze still looked a little sad, the corner of her eyes crinkled as she walked passed him.

"I promise." Adam sauntered behind her and reached for her hand. "Let's go somewhere where we can talk."

"All right."

Holding Elle's hand in his, Adam led the way into the large family room. It's fifteen feet high ceilings with large windows and wood fireplace made this room one of his favorites.

Memories took hold as he sat down on the old leather couch. Elle curled one leg under the other beside him.

"This room is my favorite in this ranch house." Adam got up and put some wood pieces in the fireplace and started a fire.

"Why's that?"

"There are so many good memories here. I still remember like it was yesterday, my great-grandmother gliding back and forth in that rocking chair near the wood stove. She crocheted large warm socks for great-grandfather regularly."

Adam looked around the room. "Grand would watch the wood burn from his large chair that faced the fireplace and blow smoke circles from his pipe. I can still smell that sweet scent whenever I come into this room. Of course, that memory is always followed by memories of great-grandmother telling him to go outside with that thing."

He grinned at her.

Elle giggled at the story. "Sounds like your great-grandparents loved well and had a lot of grace for each other's quirks."

"Yes, that they did."

"Listening to your mother talk about your father, seems like they were really close too. That's a wonderful family legacy to have."

"It is."

"It was much the same with my parents before Mom died from cancer. They loved each other so much. It was really difficult for my Dad when she passed away. It was like there was this huge hole missing from our lives, where she had been." Elle's eyes swam with tears. "Sorry, I don't mean to turn into a water faucet."

"Hey, you don't ever have to be sorry about missing those you love." Adam put his hand on hers, rubbing gently along the top of her knuckles. The simple gesture of his hand touching hers brought tingles of warmth that shot up his arm.

"Thanks for that." Elle swallowed back emotions before she continued. "Your Mom and Grandparents are so encouraging. It was great to see them tonight. They must be a big support to you and your brothers."

Adam could tell Elle was trying to shift the conversation away from herself and the family she still missed.

"They are. We do what we can to cheer them on too. Like tonight when Mom shared her story. Doing that wasn't easy for her, but she got through it." Adam studied the flickering fire light for a moment before turning toward his wife.

"She was so courageous to share her story tonight. She's an inspiration." Elle hesitated and sighed. "It must be really great to have family that is always there to encourage you. I've missed that."

"Have your Stepmother and Carly been there for you?" A furrow formed on Adam's forehead as he questioned her.

"Sadly, my Stepmother and Stepsister have never supported me like that. But I'm okay because Joanna and Bella have been there for me."

"And now you have me and my family too." Adam intertwined his fingers with hers, loving the way her small fingers fit perfectly in his.

"Yes."

There was an uncertainty in her reply Adam didn't like much. He should've expected it as he hadn't been around much in the past few days.

"Lately, I haven't really been the support you've needed." Adam leaned closer to Elle, picked up her hand and kissed it while his gaze held hers. "I am truly sorry."

She bobbed her head unspeaking, her gaze holding his.

"I'm going to change my work schedule. I'm going to ask my team to manage what they can with the beta test of that software and I'll use the rest of that time to work remotely from my office here at home." He would be happy to spend more time here, closer to Elle.

"I understand you're busy, but it would be nice to have you here." Elle yawned and put her head back against the couch. "I guess we are both going to get even busier with the renovation of the racetrack and training my new horse."

Adam moved Elle closer to him and put his arm around her shoulders. She curled up against him, and sighed.

"Yeah, it looks like it."

"I wish we could have more days that end with the two of us together like this, Adam." Elle closed her eyes and soon was fast asleep.

Adam agreed. He kissed the top of her head and pulled her close, enjoying having her near.

This time as he thought about how he'd enjoyed their evening together, he didn't have a suffocating fear which normally accompanied that thought.

He shifted a little, and picked up his wife and carried her to her bedroom. Setting her down on the bed, he covered her with a blanket.

Bending down, he kissed her forehead. A soft sigh escaped before she rolled over and went to sleep.

When he reached the door, he stood there watching her for a few minutes unsure of what was happening to him.

Maybe those old fears didn't have such a pull on him anymore. Maybe the cold shell around his heart was beginning to melt.

"ELLE, could I ask for your opinion on this?" Adam called her over to his large office.

He was talking with the landscape architect, and they

were trying to figure out the best place for the new stables Adam was adding to the new racetrack renovation.

"Sure, what is it?"

"Just wondering about your thoughts on this. Should we increase the size of the grandstand? How many stalls should we build for this racetrack?" Adam put his hand gently on the small of her back.

Touching her unexpectedly was something Adam had started doing more of lately. She liked it a little too much.

"It would encourage more people from the community and surrounding communities to use the racetrack, so yes, I think it's a good idea." Elle did her best to focus only on the question. She appreciated the fact Adam asked her opinion on details that were important to him.

"We should also have a separate entrance to the racetrack, and reserve the driveway to the ranch house, for family and friends."

"Yes. Good idea. Let's do that." They talked for a few more minutes before finalizing the plans. The landscape designer soon left to get his team ready to begin the next day.

"So the details are coming together for the racetrack then?" Elle leaned against his office desk her gaze roaming over the design.

"Yes. It's looking good. I have a bunch of workers coming tomorrow to begin the work, so that's a good start." Adam ran a hand through his hair.

Elle realized it was a nervous gesture when he was uncertain about how something would go.

"It'll be fine. The teams you hired are professionals,

and they'll do a good job." Elle put her hand on his arm to try to settle his nerves.

"I guess you're right. No need to be concerned." Adam put his hand on hers, lifted it and kissed the back of her hand. "You are a big help, do you know that?"

"I'm not sure how." Elle shrugged.

"You are able to bring calm, even when the situation seems chaotic. That's not something I do very well, so I appreciate you helping me. Especially since it seems like all these renovations and designs need our attention all at the same time." Adam lifted her other hand and kissed the back of that one too.

Elle could feel his soft lips and couldn't help but wish he was kissing her lips instead.

Heat rose from her neck to her cheeks.

A hazy memory of the night before came back. She had fallen asleep on his shoulder and woke up in her own bed.

Somewhere in between, she thought she'd dreamed of Adam's kiss on her forehead and of his gentle hands tucking the blanket around her.

"Well, I'm glad I could help." Reclaiming her hands, she slipped them into the pocket of her jeans. She didn't know what she was more afraid of, that he was kissing her hands or the fact that she was tempted to pull his head down to kiss his lips.

"Maybe you could help me a little too." Elle was desperate to find a way to get her mind off of Adam's kisses.

"Sure."

"Well, at the benefit gala, your mom introduced me to

a couple of women who are connecting me with more groups who would be interested in the horse therapy programs."

"That's great, Elle."

"Yes, it is great, but it's more than I expected. In the last two days, I've had calls or text messages from ten different crowds. Some are calling from groups with children with physical or mental disabilities, and some are organizations that are asking for horse therapy for children from poorer families."

"Then, I also have a couple of groups who are interested in horse therapy for teenagers and adults who suffer from Post Traumatic Stress Disorder." Elle started to walk back and forth across the room, trying to think it through.

"Well, sounds like you have more people interested than you originally planned for."

"That's true." Elle rubbed a hand on her forehead. "So, a couple of big questions I have now are how do I separate the different horse therapy sessions for each group and then how do I find enough people to help me handle all of this?"

"Here, let me try to map out possibilities. Sometimes it's helpful to see it drawn out." Adam sat down in the chair behind his desk and pulled out a blank sheet.

He sketched out a map to the Jennings ranch, focused on the barn and the large pasture. "Here's an idea. If we divide this pasture area that's closest to the barn into two large areas, we can fence each one off and use it specifically for horse therapy programs."

"That looks good. But now we still have to plan how to

fit each group into the week." Elle walked over and stood beside Adam, looking over his shoulder.

"Well, that shouldn't be too difficult." Adam sketched out days of the week inside each of the two areas where the horse therapy programs would run. "If you ran two programs side-by-side for four days a week and you only did it in the afternoons, you would easily be able to find room for each of the groups."

"That's so good." Elle leaned down, her blond ponytail slipping over her shoulder as she traced her finger along the drawings Adam made. "Now I can see how to better handle requests from each group. The only problem is how to find all workers I need to get this up and running. Any ideas?"

"Actually, I do. I was thinking about the community around here. There are a few teenagers and adults regularly looking for work here."

"If you set up a bunch of advertisements at the Paradise Lake Library, community center and also on the local radio, you would have a few responses. And if you don't get enough emails or calls from that, it's simple enough to expand to the surrounding communities."

"Yes. Most likely there are a few families in town who have teenagers looking for work." Elle sighed in relief as she looked down at the sketch Adam had made. She was grateful that now she had a bit of a roadmap to follow, it made getting the programs started a little easier.

Elle smiled. "The good news is that I do have a few sponsors now, thanks to the people at your benefit gala. So that should help with the extra costs of hiring workers. I have set up this Horse Therapy program as a nonprofit organization, so that should make things easier to get sponsors."

"And I would like to be one of your first sponsors."

"Oh Adam, you really don't need to do that." Elle's protests fell on deaf ears.

"I want to contribute. What you're doing is helping a lot of people, and it's something I believe in." Adam reached into his desk drawer and pulled out a check book. With a flourish, he wrote it out and handed it to her. "Here you go."

Her eyes widened at the amount. It was hundred thousand dollars. Now she could hire workers and fix up the riding area on the ranch.

Elle had a little more than half of the money that Adam gave her sitting in her bank account, but she didn't want to use that unless absolutely necessary.

The two hundred thousand dollars had paid off the rest of the mortgage, but she really hoped to pay that back too. She intended to give it back to him, as she didn't like the idea of being the poor orphan girl that Adam felt sorry for.

"Thank you, Adam. Not only did you take time out of your busy day to help me, but you also donated to this cause. I'm grateful." There had been very few people in her life that had cared enough to take extra time away from their busy lives to help her with things that were important to her.

Her husband had even taken time away from his own deadline to offer advice and support. She felt appreciated. A new awareness swept her senses of how it must feel to have someone really care for you.

Elle lowered her head intent on kissing his cheek, but he surprised her when he turned his head and looked up at her.

For a moment he paused, then his mouth closed possessively over hers, searing his name onto her heart. Placing one hand behind her head and the other on her waist, he moved his chair back and slid her onto his lap.

"Adam…" Elle started to protest, but any unwillingness on her part dissolved as his arms wrapped protectively around her. He kissed her with a fierce tenderness, shaping and fitting her lips with his own.

"Elle, you are so beautiful and perfect just the way you are. You're the best thing that's ever happened to me."

He explored the soft recesses of her mouth until she shuddered with a sensation she had never known. Elle's heart took in his words like a sponge, soaking in words she'd longed to hear all her life.

She wanted desperately to believe them.

Consuming kisses followed, and Elle felt like she was on fire. Never had she felt so willing to receive Adam's kisses.

When she was younger, there had been little time for puppy-love. Later on, there wasn't any man she cared for enough to date.

When it came to kissing and men, she was quite the innocent girl. These sensations Adam awakened in her had been dormant for far too long. Her heart was awakening to love, and she didn't know how to put a stop to it.

An insistent scratching at the office door filled the silence. Adam's impatient groan, pulled Elle out of the heady stupor of kisses.

"It's Ginger. I think she needs to go out." Elle pushed lightly against his chest and stood to her feet at the dog's loud whining.

"Next time, I'm going to make sure all dogs, cats or any other animals are far away from us." Adam stood and walked toward the door.

Heat rose up her neck to her cheeks as he mentioned a next time for his kisses.

She wouldn't know how to withstand his advances as her heart still beat wildly in her chest and her legs still felt like rubber.

"And yes, there will be a next time. I promise." Adam turned his darkened gaze to her one last time before he opened the door.

CHAPTER TEN

dam

"I'VE GOT to get to the office. The team is having issues that I need to look into and help problem solve."

"All right." Elle watched as her husband hurried to put his coffee cup by the sink before slipping on his oxford shoes.

He wore a white dress shirt with the top button open and a navy-blue sports jacket over top of his light brown dress pants.

A couple of curls stuck out from his collar. Elle itched to straighten them out, but resisted.

She held his computer case and Adam gave her a quick kiss before reaching for it.

"I wish I could stay, but I can't. The beta version of this software could be delayed if we don't work out these problems now. It's scheduled to release in five days." Adam walked toward the door and frowned. "I might be home late. We'll have to see how it goes today."

"No worries. Just get it fixed." Elle waved at him as he left the house. She grinned at the sound of her own 'wife-like' words.

His kisses yesterday still made her toes curl, and her heart raced faster as she remembered. He had been thoughtful last night too when he offered to make supper for the two of them.

Sighing she realized she would really miss Adam today. But he needed to get the problems solved with that software, there was no two ways about it.

Besides, she had so much to do. There were new workers showing up today that needed to be trained. She would need to organize the construction workers who were creating two horse therapy training areas on her Dad's ranch.

Hurriedly, she slipped her hoodie over her head and stepped outside, Ginger at her heels.

The loud roar from the machine's engine assaulted Elle's ears as she hurried from the ranch house. It was exciting to see the new irrigation system alongside the new paddocks for the horses.

It was really good to see Adam happy and one of his dreams being fulfilled. She hoped she got a chance to help him realize many other dreams.

"YOU'LL BE sure to have him at the ranch by mid-afternoon then?" Adam smiled as he heard the man on the other end of the phone line go on and on. "Good. See you this afternoon then. Thanks."

Adam fist pounded the air in his excitement. Elle was going to have her big surprise today after all.

For almost a week, he'd been really head down, getting his software ready to launch.

He had started organizing everything last week for Elle's birthday. But then, with all the problems he'd had with getting the security software ready to go, he'd let things slide.

Adam had forgot to tell his assistant about the changes he made to Elle's birthday party until she had already left for home. Getting the details ready for this important moment couldn't wait. So, he found himself on the phone for the last hour, trying to get things ready for this afternoon.

He sighed in relief. Now that it was done, he could go home.

Adam drove back to the ranch, his mind on Elle. In the past week, she had been able to get a lot done at her Dad's ranch. He was proud of her for stepping out of her comfort zone to hire people to help with the horse therapy programs.

He drove up the long drive to the ranch house, glad to be back home. As he got out of the car, he looked around, grateful that the machines were no longer renovating and digging up dirt.

Adam walked to where the new stables were being constructed. These stables along with the grandstand were about halfway to completion with plans to finish them in the next two weeks.

He turned toward the race track, noticing how the packed dirt had been harrowed over. It was in top shape, ready to hold its first race.

Grinning, Adam looked heavenward, hoping that Grand was looking down and smiling. Great-grandfather had talked about renovating the race track for years, saying he wanted to do something his grandchildren and the surrounding community could enjoy.

Adam was glad this first phase of the project was almost complete.

Just as he rounded the corner and walked toward the rails along the track, he heard the sound of horse hooves.

Looking up, his gaze took in his dark brown quarter horse galloping around the final curve of the race track toward the finish line. Elle sat crouched on the horse's back, her hands hanging onto the reins, her blond ponytail flying out behind her.

She flew past him.

His heart stopped in his chest. His wife was going much too fast. Someone would need to remind her that it wasn't safe.

Adam jumped over the rail and walked toward Elle who had slowed the horse down to a slow trot. She tugged on the reins to ease into a walk as she saw him.

"That was so much fun." Elle wiped wisps of hair away from her face and grinned. She patted the horse's neck. "I realize Beauty here isn't a thoroughbred but she didn't seem to mind the run. I hope you don't mind that I took her out?"

"What I wish is that you would slow down when you ride." Adam's tone came out sharper than he intended. The muscles in her face tightened and her lips formed a thin line. He looked up at her and regretted the harsh words.

She stared at him in silence for a moment.

"I'm sorry, Adam. I wasn't trying to overwork her. She really wanted to run today." Elle grabbed the mane and slowly slid off the horse. Adam caught her in his arms and embraced her close.

"No, I'm sorry. I shouldn't have spoken to you like I did." He kissed the top of her head enjoying having her near. "I just want you to be safe, that's all."

"I know you do." She sighed and looked up at him, confusion still evident in her eyes.

"Forgive me?" Adam felt like a jerk. Seeing her flying down the track, knowing the danger she was in, nearly stopped his heart. He'd been terrified.

He had to get past these stupid fears he had. It was always there, just hovering on the edge, whenever someone he cared for was exposed to the possibility of danger.

He had to stop overreacting. Problem was he didn't know how.

"Of course." Elle hugged him and planted a light kiss on his lips.

"That kiss was much too short. I need to give you a happy birthday kiss that you'll remember." Adam lowered his head and with a whispered *happy birthday sweetheart,* his lips sought hers.

His arms circled her protectively, drawing her gently

against his hard chest. Her mouth was moist and pliant against his own.

Again and again he kissed her with a fierce tenderness, almost like he was afraid she'd disappear from his arms.

The loud crackling of tire wheels on rocks brought Adam out of his kiss-induced stupor. He lifted his head to see his family had arrived.

It was time for the birthday fun to begin.

&

"Happy birthday, Elle!" Adam's mother drew her into a warm hug.

Tears pricked the back of Elle's eyes as more family members hugged and kissed her cheek.

"Oh, my goodness. What a wonderful birthday surprise!" Elle's gaze turned to see each member of Adam's family smiling back at her. "It's been years since I had anyone throw me a birthday party."

"You're behind this." She turned her head to look up at Adam.

"Guilty." His mouth twitched with mischief.

"Thank you so much." Elle hugged him and swallowed back tears that threatened to overflow.

Memories of her last birthday party whirled in her head. She had been ten years old. It was the last year when it had been just her and her dad.

He had surprised her by bringing over three friends from school, and it had been such a fun day with cake, presents and playing games together.

Today, she felt appreciated and loved just like she had on that day so many years ago.

Before long, Joanna arrived, Bella by her side.

"Happy Birthday, you." Bella threw her arms around her and Joanna did the same.

"I'm liking this surprise birthday more and more."

"Well, I didn't want to miss this one. You've had too many years where you've spent your birthday working with no one to celebrate you. From now on, things are going to be different." Joanna put her arm around Elle's waist.

"I don't feel like I deserve all this love and attention, but I'm grateful for it anyway." Elle murmured. The caterers were busy laying the food and cake out on the table.

Adam and his family sat on the chaise lounge set with its plush cushions on the large outside deck, drinking cool drinks and laughing together.

"Listen, my darling girl. You deserve every bit of this attention. And Adam is a lucky man to have you for his wife. His family is lucky to have you too."

"You make me want to believe it, Joanna." A familiar nagging doubt coiled at the pit of Elle's stomach. She didn't think she'd ever be good enough to truly fit into Adam's world. It was a good thing she was only his fake wife, and not a real one.

"Good, you should believe it." Joanna stopped suddenly, her gaze direct and piercing. "Listen to me. It's all those years of being told you weren't good enough by Lilleth that has you believing those lies. You're more than good enough. You are beautiful inside and out."

"What would I do without you to talk sense into me? You always seem to know how to make me feel better." She sighed as she thought of her stepmother. "But, I'll admit, it's always been a battle with her. This past week was another one."

"What happened?"

"Lilleth was angry when a bunch of new workers showed up for training to help with the horse therapy programs. My stepmother doesn't want me to keep the nonprofit on the ranch. She told me she's going to figure out a way to put a stop to it. I don't know what to do because the situation keeps getting worse." Elle's shoulders drooped.

"Well, just wait it out then. However, there might come a day when you might need to either find some other land for your horse therapy programs, or find a way to fully own your Dad's ranch." Joanna shook her head and sighed.

"Yeah, I had the same thought. Well, I'm not going to think about that today. Today is about having fun." Elle looped her arms in Joanna and Belle's as they walked together to the outside lounge area.

"You're just in time." Adam pulled out the chair beside him. Elle sat down as the caterers brought a chef salad which was soon followed by different kinds of chicken and ham wraps, crab cakes and potato cakes with smoked salmon.

"How is it going with your nonprofit program? Eliza mentioned that you had some new groups who were interested." Adam's grandmother sat across from her looking elegant in an ivory colored three-quarter length knit shirt and tailored Navy-blue pants. Elle admired Catherine's simple elegance every time she saw her.

"It's going good. Thanks to Eliza, I've had more requests from organizations in the past week than I've ever had. It's looking to be a busy summer." Elle took a sip of her water.

"Maybe when things slow down a little, we can have that spa day just for us girls." Catherine winked at her.

"It'll probably slow down in the fall, we can plan the details then."

"That would be wonderful. I really want to get to know my new granddaughter better."

"I'd love that."

Elle, looked around at everyone gathered at the table, amazed that she could be a part of this large and loving family.

To be surrounded by a loving family was something she'd always dreamed of, but never really thought it would happen for her.

Not for the first time, she wondered if it were possible for her relationship with Adam to become real.

As they finished lunch, Elle heard Bella's sweet voice singing happy birthday and everyone joined in.

She had just blown out the candles when a truck drove up the driveway.

"Did you invite someone else to the party?" Elle grinned up at Adam.

"Yes." Adam's eyes grew a little wider and he grabbed her hand. "Come and meet our new guest."

Elle followed Adam down the steps and onto the gravel driveway that led to the barn.

A man got out of the truck and walked to the trailer behind it.

"Here he is." He opened the gate to the horse trailer, and gently tugged on a rope.

Elle's eyes widened as she saw her horse walk down the ramp.

"Justice is here." Elle breathed out his name, a little in awe to see the race horse Adam had given her standing in front of her.

"Do you like this horse as much as you did a few weeks ago?" The teasing tone in Adam's voice made her smile.

"I love him even more if that's possible." She stood there for a moment just staring at her horse before turning to her husband. "Oh Adam, what a beautiful birthday gift. Thank you." Elle gave her husband a quick hug and then turned to walk slowly toward her new horse.

Justice stood there, looking majestic and radiant. According to the previous owner, he measured at seventeen hands tall. He was among the tallest thoroughbreds in racing.

His sleek dark brown coat and black mane glowed in the afternoon sun. His dark brown eyes looked alert.

Elle reached her hand to his neck, enjoying the silky smooth coat.

In her mind, Justice was powerful, bold and courageous.

Elle looked forward to feeling more of that as she rode Justice.

Taking the halter, she walked him toward the pasture, focused on getting her new horse settled in his new surroundings.

"I look forward to seeing him race." Elle turned to see Adam's Granddad step beside her. Adam walked on his other side.

"You should have seen Justice run at the Royal Ascot, Granddad. He was incredible." Adam went on to talk about all the races they saw there.

"Sounds like you got the pick of the lot."

"We really did." Adam opened the gate and Elle walked Justice into the pasture area where the grass grew green and full. She unhooked the halter and left him free to roam.

"He's finally home." Elle locked the gate, and they all stood together watching the new horse wander through the pasture, eating as he went.

"Yeah, and after he's settled in and the race track is finished, we'll start with a horse trainer to get him ready for this year's races."

"I'd like to see this race track of yours up close, Adam." Granddad walked with them toward the construction area.

"I'm happy with how much has been done already." Adam began to explain the plan to his grandfather. The track had been lengthened to a mile and a quarter and it was now wider as well.

The fence along the race track included rubber pads along the rails and posts. The construction on the much larger grandstand was progressing. All was coming together.

"You've done well." Granddad clapped him on the back. "Pop was right about you Adam. I didn't see it, but he did. He said you loved this ranch and horses as much as he did. It was one of his dreams to give the ranch to someone who had a love for the place, and who loved horse racing and the community like he did."

Elle watched as Adam swallowed a few times before answering. She could tell he was moved by his grandfather's words.

"Thanks Granddad. It means a lot to hear you say that."

"And now you've married a gal who loves the horses like you do. Seems to me, like it's a match made in heaven." He grinned at his own wit.

Eliza walked up to the fence and stood beside Elle.

Before long, Adam and his grandfather wandered off to look more closely at the new renovations happening by the grandstand and stables.

"It's so wonderful to be back here at the old homestead, especially for my only daughter-in-law's birthday." Eliza gently bumped into Elle's shoulder, a half smile on her face.

"I'm so glad you came."

"We wouldn't miss it. You are important to Adam, and that means you're also important to me and to the rest of the family."

A longing rose up in Elle at her mother-in-law's words. She wished she could be really sure that she was important to Adam.

His surprise birthday party and buying that beautiful horse should've made her realize her importance to him. She would hold onto that.

Maybe her marriage to Adam could become a real one.

Maybe her husband could fall in love with her, like she was falling for him.

Maybe their marriage would grow into what Adam's grandfather believed it was — a match made in Heaven.

CHAPTER ELEVEN

dam

ADAM WALKED BESIDE HIS WIFE, tucking her hand in his arm as they descended from the Stevenson private jet and walked to the waiting car.

They had flown to Barbados for a business dinner with Houston born tech guru, Bobby Michael.

Bobby's massive private estate was along the waterfront and quite beautiful.

It wasn't long before their driver stopped the car in front of the mansion near where many large yachts were docked.

"Thanks for coming today." Adam whispered and held out his arm as they got out of the car.

Elle's green eyes glowed in the shimmer of lights that

surrounded the pier. Ruby red earrings swayed from her delicate ears, their twinkling shine reflecting in her eyes.

"I'm happy to be with you Adam. Although I must admit to feeling intimidated and out of my element tonight." Elle whispered in his ear.

"There's no need to feel uncomfortable. Just be yourself." Adam put his hand on the small of her back as they made their way up to the double front steps.

As Elle walked beside him, Adam admired her beauty. Her long blond hair was done up in a French twist that revealed her slender neck.

The red dress she wore swept down to her tiny waist and floated gracefully around her legs as she walked. His wife was a combination of compassion, intelligence and beauty. In his business circles she was a rare gem.

He really didn't expect Elle to come to all his business functions. She was busy enough without adding another item to her list.

For tonight he was grateful to have his beautiful wife by his side. For tonight he needed to be focused.

Tonight, he needed to concentrate on being the devoted husband, and honest businessman he was.

As soon as they stepped onto the deck of the yacht, their host met them.

"Ah, Adam Stevenson. It is good of you to join us tonight." Bobby Michael shook his hand.

"It's good to be here, Bobby." Adam shook his hand.

"And this must be your lovely wife?"

"Yes, this is my wife, Elle." Elle's cheeks flushed a lovely pink as the man bowed slightly over her hand.

"Please, come inside." Bobby led them to a large sitting

area with sofas in soft white gracing three sides of the massive room.

Drink tables were set out on either side of the large space. At the far end of the room behind a glass wall perched on top of a glass fireplace, sat a large mahogany table that seated at least twenty people.

Large windows lined the wall on either side, filling the room with light and making the space even larger.

Many men and women that he'd come to meet were scattered around the room, sitting and talking.

"Welcome. Please, let one of my servers prepare your favorite drink and make yourself at home." Bobby waved one of the waiters over to them.

As Bobby welcomed other guests, Adam and Elle took a moment for themselves.

A crease formed between Adam's brows as his gaze swept the room. He would need to focus and somehow manage to talk one or two people who would be good connections for his business.

"I see you worrying." Elle squeezed his hand, getting his attention. His wife whispered as they walked into the ballroom.

Adam stood motionless for a moment, his gaze roaming over the crowd of business people in the room.

The large room was crowded, the waiters busy going back and forth with their trays.

"I am wondering who I should talk to first. I'm looking for someone who can help expand our new software into larger markets." Adam glanced at the man with silver streaks in his black hair. He wore a navy suit with a red tie. "Over there is Andreas Christakos. He has a lot of connections in the European markets."

Adam then nodded at an Asian man whose hands were busy moving up and down as he talked with another conservatively dressed man. "Over there is Nian Zhen, who is an important connection to the Asian markets. I think I'll talk to him first."

He was surrounded by three men and women, talking animatedly about something. "I am going to go chat with some of them. Wander around and enjoy yourself, Elle."

"I'll do my best." Elle's gaze shifted to the other people in the room.

From the uncertain look in her eyes and how she squirmed beside him, he could tell being here tonight was very uncomfortable for her.

"You're beautiful." Adam whispered in her ear.

Her gaze met his, uncertainty clouding her expression.

"You're going to be fine." He took her hand, and moved his thumb in small circles across the delicate skin of her wrist. "Relax."

"Thank you." Elle sighed, relief evident in her eyes.

He lifted her hand and brushed a soft kiss against her knuckles. "I'll be here whenever you need me." The corners of her mouth turned up into a dreamy smile while a sprinkle of pink blossomed in her cheeks.

Adam drew in a shaky breath. If this meeting wasn't so important, if he hadn't promised his brothers, he'd take his wife somewhere private and explore the sweet shape of her mouth for hours.

But tonight, he had a job to do. "I'm going to talk to Nian Zhen. Wish me luck." Adam squeezed her hand and walked toward the man from China who now stood alone. He was going to make the most of this opportunity.

He hoped Elle would be able to relax enough to enjoy the evening.

§

ELLE WATCHED Adam walk away from her and immediately missed his company.

She clung to his encouraging words but insecurity still taunted her.

Looking out over the crowded room caused another wave of self-doubt to roll over her. The large room was filled with men and women who were dressed to impress, talking easily with one another.

This world of glitz and glamour was familiar to Adam but felt awkward and uncomfortable to her.

Yet, this was part of what she'd agreed to when they made their marriage pact. She needed to hold up her end of their agreement.

You can do this. You can make small talk with strangers. You can get to know some of these people who are important to Adam.

With a new determination, she pulled her shoulders back and walked toward the drink table. Picking up a lemon water, she walked towards the group of people who had gathered around Andreas Christakos.

The Greek businessman was talking about the latest trends in the European markets. As Elle listened, she took note of Andreas's interests in case she had a chance to talk to him later.

It wasn't long before the group went their separate ways.

Elle had a moment alone to talk with Andreas. He was easy to talk with and seemed interested in Adam's security software.

Before long, Elle turned her attention to search for the tech guru from Texas.

Spotting him over by the art pieces at the other end of the large room, she squared her shoulders and walked toward him.

Meandering her way through a group of people, she reached the alcove where many incredible paintings hung on the wall.

Her gaze lingered on each painting one by one, taking small sips of her drink as she appreciated the artwork.

Staring at a Picasso painting of a boy leading his horse, she admired the detail of light and shadows.

"You must be an admirer of beautiful art." A deep voice whispered in her ear.

She glanced up to see Bobby Michael looking at her, a playful light in his brown eyes.

His imposing height and the high quality business suit he wore gave him a commanding presence, but his voice was light-hearted.

Elle inhaled a deep breath and blew it out slowly relaxing her hands at her sides.

"Yes, I love art. Especially art that features horses or children. The two just seem to fit together." Elle looked up at the tall man beside her whose dark eyes gazed down at her with a mischievous twinkle.

"What is it about horses or children that you find so captivating?"

"With horses that's easy." Elle stepped a little closer to the painting. "You can see the horse's shoulder and flank outlined in detail by the way the artist played with light and shadows. I think it illustrates the power and strength of the horse."

"And with children?"

"With children, it's their innocence and passion for life that draws me." Elle looked at the painting again, thinking about the children who came every week to the ranch for the horse therapy program.

"Children are amazing in their ability to heal from painful wounds, to forgive and rebound from the past. I think this painting showcases a little of that."

"So much insight and passion from one so young. You appreciate the artist's attention to detail?" Bobby leaned in to the painting to get a closer look at the details.

"I do."

"I can appreciate that. For instance, in this painting I see how the light shines between the boy and his horse, and it reminds me of the light in your beautiful green eyes — shining with a secret delight." Mr. Michael's eyes gleamed and a smile dangled on the corner of his lips.

"Thank you." Elle's cheeks flushed unsure of how to respond.

She searched the room for her husband before turning back to Bobby.

"Are you and Adam newly married?" His mouth quirked up at their corners.

"Yes."

"Tell me again about Adam's business interests?"

"I'd be happy to explain what I know," Elle began. "Adam created a new security software which has received great reviews from tech companies in Silicon Valley. In fact, I think you would appreciate what he has created, Bobby. From what I understand you have interests in the software industry."

"I do." He didn't go on. Elle made a mental note to nudge Adam to do a little more digging into Bobby's interests, so Adam could get to know him and come to a mutual understanding.

"I haven't had the pleasure of getting to know your husband."

"You will soon I'm sure."

"Perhaps." Mr. Michael's dark brown eyes once again fastened on hers, and he gave her a winsome smile. "But, Mrs. Stevenson, I hope we can be friends."

"Yes, I'd like that."

"I'm glad." He held out his arm. "Why don't you tell me more about your passion for horses as I escort you back to the dinner table."

Elle slipped her hand into the crook of his arm and walked with him out of the alcove. "That might take a longer walk. The short version is, I've had a passion for horses since I was a little girl. I love to ride horses, and enjoy watching them race. Since my husband bought me a race horse a few weeks ago, I'm excited to see him run."

"Ah, horse racing. That does sound exciting."

"It is. Horse racing is the best kind of fun." Elle looked up at Bobby and they shared a smile as they neared the dinner table. Many people had already sat down.

She spotted Adam seated at the dinner table, waiting for her. Her husband's gaze was cool and distant.

Mr. Michaels led her to Adam and pulled out the chair next to him. "It's time for us to sit down for dinner. I hope you both enjoy the meal."

Bobby walked toward the head of the dinner table, and sat down.

Dinner was filled with small talk, but Elle was anxious for it to be over. Her stomach had been clenched tight throughout dinner because of the chilly response from her husband.

She breathed a sigh of relief when the meal was finished and many people stood up to walk around.

Adam stood to his feet and held his arm out for her.

Seeing their host they made their way toward him, Elle said. "Mr. Michaels. Thank you for a lovely evening."

"Of course. It was my pleasure." Mr. Michaels turned to Adam."Before you go, I wanted to tell you I heard high praise tonight about the security software you've created. Perhaps we could schedule a time to meet and you could tell me more about it?"

"That would be good. You can find my contact information on my website here." Adam pulled out his card. He seemed to be doing his best to keep things professional even though she could hear his cool tone of voice.

"Thanks again. I'll be in touch." Adam nodded.

At that moment an idea sprouted and Elle thought it might help Adam.

"Just to let you know, we're having our first horse race on the new track at the ranch in a few weeks. Would you care to join us, Bobby?"

"Yes, that would be wonderful. Thank you for the invitation Elle."

"I'll let you know the date of the event." Elle sent him a warm smile.

"That would be good. I look forward to it."

Adam walked towards the door, Elle by his side.

He helped her with her jacket, then hurried outside to their waiting car. Not much was said between them until they were finally settled in the plane, ready for the flight home.

Finally, Elle needed a conversation between them.

"Adam, you seem cold and distant. Is something wrong?"

Adam sighed. "I am frustrated with myself that I asked you to get to know people tonight… especially the businessmen. It was annoying to watch."

Elle folded her arms in front of her, uncertain what she could say to that.

Adam loosened his tie and pulled it off.

He grunted. "And, I wish you wouldn't have invited Mr. Michaels to the horse racing event. I don't want him showing up at the ranch."

Elle sighed, confusion flooding her about her new husband. "I invited him because I thought it would be good for your business." Tears pricked the back of her eyes, wondering how this evening had gone south so fast.

"How do you think it would be good for business?" Adam's forehead crinkled like it did when he doubted something.

"Because I know." Elle shrugged. "Just like I have an

instinct about when a horse is ready for the next step in the training process, I have a similar instinct about people. If you would simply have a friendly conversation with Mr. Michaels, he would come around and give you what you want."

"Maybe."

Adam's cool gaze met hers, making her wonder if he would ever see reason.

She waited for him to say something else, but he was silent, continuing to be distant. It looked like this conversation would need to wait.

"Since you don't seem to feel like talking tonight, I'll say good night." Elle whispered and walked towards the bedroom at the back of the plane.

Lying on the bed wide awake, she was fairly certain a peaceful sleep would be hard won this night.

ADAM SAT on the comfortable leather chair of the plane, his fingers shaky as they combed through his hair.

As he thought about the evening, the truth hit him hard. He was jealous — through and through.

He'd been in the wrong and needed to fix things with his wife. Adam realized he would need to apologize in the morning.

Adam's fingers shook slightly as they combed through his hair.

Standing to his feet, he poured himself a cup of coffee from the sidebar and sat down.

Positioning his laptop on the table in front of him, he decided to work — fairly certain he wouldn't sleep much this night.

CHAPTER TWELVE

Elle

ALL NIGHT long Elle had tossed and turned.

The argument she'd had with Adam last night had irritated and confused her, and she needed a way to release some of that pent-up frustration.

The plane had landed a couple of hours ago and Adam had already gone to his office.

They hadn't spoken except for polite conversation.

A ride on her horse was just what she needed.

Today, it seemed like her horse also suffered from too much energy.

"It's okay, boy." Elle patted Justice's neck as she walked him out onto the new race track. She needed to ride today.

She'd started working with Justice as soon as he arrived, so her horse was used to her.

Working with their new horse trainer, Jed Lee, she had begun to understand the best way to train her new horse. It had really helped her understand commands and the importance of the positions of her hands and legs too.

Today she wasn't focused on training though.

Today she just wanted to ride. Fast.

Gripping the thoroughbred's mane, Elle quickly slid onto the saddle. Guiding the horse out of the barn, she led him down the dirt track.

The morning sun shone down on the freshly harrowed dirt. She was glad she was by herself this morning. Adam had left for his office before breakfast so she didn't even see him this morning.

She needed time to think before they talked again.

Reaching the starting line, she set the small timer in her pocket so she could time how fast her horse galloped around a mile and a quarter track.

Justice paced along the rail line, his nose high in the wind. His mane fluttered with his tail raised high, almost like he was showing off.

Elle grinned at his eagerness to run today.

Slipping the pocket watch inside her closely fitted jacket, she gave the horse his head and urged him onward.

Justice's powerful legs surged forward and soon they were flying down the track. She hung on tight to his mane and put her head down close to his neck so she could just see above his head.

She loved the sense of freedom as she sat on the back of her race horse and saw the full length of track ahead.

The horse's heart raced beneath her hands, each full breath lifting her slightly from her seat as he lunged forward beat by beat.

In this moment she felt like she could be or do anything. In this moment it felt like mistakes she had made or arguments she had were wiped clean. In this moment a new beginning seemed possible.

Rounding the final corner along the track, she saw the flag for the finish line and urged Justice to go a little faster.

They crossed the finish line and Elle couldn't help but feel a sense of victory. It was a strange feeling, since they weren't racing against any other horse.

She was still grinning as she slowed her horse down to a trot and turned him back to home. As she looked along the rails, Jed caught her eye and waved her over.

"You gave him a good run." Jed looked up at her and showed her the timer in his hand. "I clocked his time at just a little over two minutes."

"Wow, that really is good. He must have been ready to run today." Elle patted his neck pleased Justice had reached the average time for most thoroughbreds.

There was a reason that the Kentucky Derby called itself 'the greatest two minutes in sports.' That was around the average time it took for race horses to run the mile and a quarter track.

"Maybe he'll run better with his jockey. Is Teddy going to train on Justice today?" Elle asked about the Jockey they had hired for the upcoming races.

"He'll be here this afternoon, but I don't think he's going to beat your time."

Elle slid off the horse, handing the reins to Jed. "That's okay. Some days it seems Justice is more eager for a run than others. It's the regular training that helps keep him fit."

"Well, we're doing our best, Mrs. Stevenson."

"You're doing great. Thanks, Jed." Elle stood there watching as Jed led her horse back to the stables for a good rub down, water and food.

As she walked back to the ranch house, her thoughts turned back to Adam. She wondered if they would be able to talk today. Part of her wanted the difficult conversation while another part of her wanted to avoid it altogether.

However for right now, Elle was happy to be spending the morning with Bella.

As she walked into the yard, Elle saw her stepmother's car drive up to the house. She braced herself for what was sure to be another difficult conversation.

"I need to talk to you." Lilleth stepped out of her car and slammed the door.

Elle stood there for a full minute without saying a word. It was incredible that Lilleth could arrive somewhere and start off angry.

"Hello, Stepmother. Would you care for something cool to drink?" Elle forced herself to be courteous.

"No, I don't. And never mind acting all 'lady of the manor' with me. Remember I know you. You're nothing but the daughter of a dirt-poor rancher who died without fulfilling his promises. You're just the same as him — a wannabe who won't amount to anything."

The woman stood with her hands on her hips, her

brown eyes, steely. "I'm guessing Adam has already figured out what a poor choice he made for a wife and regrets that decision."

Elle swallowed back tears at her stepmother's hateful words.

"I don't care for your insults. If that's all that you came to tell me, then you can go ahead and leave." Elle walked toward the stairs to the house, when her stepmother spoke again.

"Not so fast. There was one other small detail I wanted to mention." Lilleth's tone changed to syrupy sweetness, which from past experience meant she had done something completely awful.

"I've put the ranch up for sale. I've already got two offers, so most likely it won't take long before it's sold. I just wanted to let you know. You need to make plans to get those horses and anything else from your therapy programs off the ranch within the next couple weeks."

Elle stood motionless, shocked into silence for a moment before she found her voice.

"You are selling my Dad's ranch? But, we just paid off the mortgage." It was all she could do to control her anger and not lash out.

"It's time for Carly and I to move somewhere new, somewhere where there won't be any reminders of the mistakes of my past." Her stepmother's cold eyes swept over her and she got into her car.

"Wait…" Elle started to speak, but Lilleth was already driving away.

Elle crumpled to the stairs a cold chill running down

her back. Her legs started to shake and she hugged her knees staring sightlessly across the yard.

She swallowed back the sting of tears at being rejected once again.

Elle knew Lilleth referred to herself as one of the mistakes from her past that she wanted to be rid of. All she'd ever wanted was to have a real mother who loved her.

Since her mother died when she was five, she had longed for the love of a mother. She longed for some kind word, some encouragement from her stepmother. She longed to finally belong.

But, it wasn't to be. Her stepmother didn't offer her that. All she got from Lilleth, were nasty comments about how she was a failure and the mistakes she made.

Maybe her stepmother was right. Maybe Adam already regretted his poor choice of a bride. She was sure he would be quite happy when the year was up for their fake marriage.

At the sound of a vehicle driving toward the house, Elle quickly wiped away the tears from her cheeks on her sleeve. It was Bella.

Her friend got out, wearing her usual jeans and a dark grey cardigan that she had tossed over a pink t-shirt.

"Hey you." Bella walked up to her and gave her a hug. "What's wrong?"

"Hey, I'm glad you're here." Elle embraced her best friend a little longer than usual, grateful for how supportive she was. "My stepmother stopped by and announced she has decided to sell the ranch."

"Oh Elle, I'm so sorry." Bella sat down beside her on the stairs.

"Yeah, me too." Elle bit her lip, doing her best to stop the flow of more tears. "So, it looks like I'll be busy for the next couple of weeks trying to find a new home for the horses and the therapy program."

"Why don't you ask Adam for the money to buy your Dad's ranch?" Bella gave Elle a confident look as if the answer was right in front of her. "It's perfect."

"No, it's not." Elle shook her head. "I won't give him yet another reason to believe I'm only after his money, or that once again he needs to rescue his pitiful wife. I can't do it, Bella. I just can't."

"Okay. Then we'll figure out another way." Bella put an arm around her shoulders, hugging her close. "We'll put our heads together and come up with something."

"Your support and friendship means so much, thank you Bella." Elle hugged her back sighing deeply.

"Always there for you, Elle, you know that."

"I do and I'm grateful."

"Do you want to stay home today instead of coming with me?"

"No. It will help to get my mind off my own problems." Elle stood to her feet. "I'll just change out of my riding gear and into jeans."

"Sure." Bella sat on the steps and started scrolling through her smartphone while Elle hurried into the house to change. Finding a pair of jeans and a green cable knit ribbed long sweater, she quickly changed.

Taking her hair out of its long ponytail, she brushed it

out and let her strawberry blond hair hang down her back.

Elle hurried outside and soon they were driving toward Seattle.

"Thanks for coming with me to the Safe House today. Your new friend Dani really likes talking with you. She's always asking for your help when they come to the ranch for horse therapy." Elle glanced at Bella.

"I like her too. I can't help but remember, if someone hadn't rescued me, I could very well be in Dani's shoes today." Bella's voice trembled and she gripped the steering wheel tighter.

"I'm grateful too." Elle thought back to that day years ago. It had been a scary time. "Maybe that's why we're committed to seeing these girls."

"Yeah."

"You would have appreciated listening to Adam's Mom's story at the benefit gala a few weeks ago." Elle shared Eliza's story with Bella.

"Wow, she really is an inspiration."

"Yes, she is."

"Speaking of the Stevenson family, how are things going with your husband?" Bella navigated through the busy streets of Seattle as she spoke.

"Not good."

"What happened?"

"Last night's business dinner, went horribly wrong." Elle told Bella what happened. "Now, Adam is angry with me because I talked with Bobby Michaels and had a great conversation with him."

"It sounds to me like Adam is jealous of Bobby. *Ooo,*

this is getting good. I might need to grab me some popcorn…" Bella winked at her and giggled.

"That is so not funny. This isn't a soap opera, this is my life we're talking about here." Elle rubbed the back of her neck. "I just don't understand."

"Okay, I'm sorry. I won't tease." Bella parked her truck on the street beside the Stevenson's BeSafe Foundation SafeHouse and reached for her hand.

"Here's what I think is going on. I'd bet your bottom dollar Adam is jealous of your easy-going conversation with the tech guru from Houston. I think last night, your husband was acting cool because he was jealous. What I think is Adam really wants you for more than just his fake wife and doesn't know how to tell you."

Elle thought about it for a moment and shook her head. As much as she wished Adam would see her as his real wife, she didn't have any delusions when it came to their relationship. Especially when memories of last night lingered in her mind.

"Hmm, I really don't think so. Not when I remember the argument we had last night."

"Maybe Adam's anger is really a cover up for fear. His heart is starting to open up to you and, it terrifies him." Bella's pointed look zeroed in on her own.

"I don't think so."

"Well, what are you going to do?"

"I'm going to tell him we should go back to just being friends and leave the messy emotions out of it. I'm just too afraid that this fake marriage can't end up anywhere but in heartache."

"If that's what you want." Bella squeezed her hand.

"It's how it has to be."

"Well, I believe you're making a mistake."

"Maybe, but I don't think so." Elle sighed, her heart in her throat. She looked up at the house. "We should probably get inside. Most likely, the girls are waiting for us." They got out of the truck and walked up the sidewalk to a large old Victorian house that had been renovated to make it into a Safe House.

Recently, Adam mentioned they had bought the house next door also because they were running out of room in the original Safe House.

Elle and Bella hurried up the steps and knocked. One of the dayworkers opened the door.

"You're here to talk to Dani and Bree right?" She quickly closed the door and locked it. "I'll send them to the downstairs kitchen and dining room. You can talk to them there."

"All right. Thanks." Elle and Bella followed her downstairs through a smaller kitchen with a door that led to the backyard garden.

They didn't wait long. Bree and Dani walked into the dining room and sat down across from them. Bella stood and Dani followed her to grab a coffee from the kitchen.

"How are you doing?" Elle barely recognized Bree as the shivering girl she had found in their shed a few weeks ago. Her cheeks had filled out to a healthy pink color. Bree's brown hair had taken on a new glow and her big brown eyes sparkled with animation and life.

"I feel good." Bree pulled her sweater around her shoulders.

"You look great."

Bella sat two cups of coffee on the table. "We're going to take a little walk. Back soon."

"Sure." Elle waved them off and took a sip of her coffee.

"Why do you and your friend come here every week? Why do you bother with me and Dani?" As usual Bree spoke what was on her mind.

"Well, the truth is that when Bella and I were in High School, Bella was kidnapped and then saved from a human trafficking operation."

"What happened?"

"Both Bella and I were at a science fair with her father. Her father is an inventor so he goes to these science fairs and conventions regularly." Elle took a deep breath before she continued.

"One night we were on our way back to the hotel from the science fair, when two men ran out from a dark alley and grabbed both me and Bella. I kicked and screamed and eventually managed to get away but poor Bella was dragged off into that dark alley."

"I ran back into the Science building and a young friend of Bella's Dad said he would try to bring her back. I ran with him and showed him where they'd taken her. I didn't think he would be able to find Bella. But, he did save her even though he was injured."

"I'm grateful to be here." Bree toyed with her hair. "The doctors that have come here have really helped me change the way I see myself so that I'm starting to believe I'm worthy of a better life."

"I'm glad." Elle smiled at the happy glow on Bree's face.

"When Adam announced a week ago that Stevenson

BeSafe foundation would pay for the first full year of college or any classes that would help people develop skills for their future, I was excited. Now it seems like this might be possible for me."

"You can do it, Bree." Elle shifted forward in her chair as she thought it through. "Adam said they would pay for college. I didn't realize that. That's very generous."

"Yeah, it's great. They're also buying a second large van to use to take people back and forth between doctor's appointments, grocery shopping and to college."

"That's really helpful."

"Yeah, so I think I might study to become a nurse. That's something I'd like to do." Bree looked up at her a flicker of uncertainty in her eyes.

"You will make a wonderful nurse, Bree."

"Thanks. It's a lot of work, but I think I can..." Bree stopped mid-sentence as her gaze shifted toward the door.

Elle turned around to see Adam leaning against the doorframe, the corners of his mouth turned up as he stared at them. His tie was loose around his collar and his hair was rumpled, as though he'd stroked a hand through it many times.

In spite of her frustration with Adam, her heart still ached for him when he had a bad day. She should steer clear of him but right now, she just wanted to savor his nearness.

She couldn't even look in his direction without revealing everything that was stored in her heart. She loved him, and she wasn't sure how she could hide that from him much longer.

So, just how was she going to be able to stick with her decision to tell him they needed to go back to being just friends?

He walked toward them.

"Hi Bree." Adam gave her a hi-five.

"Hey Adam. I was just telling Elle about doing some schooling to become a nurse."

"That's great. You'll be a good one." Bree blushed with Adam's confidence in her.

"Hey, cowgirl." His blue eyes stared at her softly, and his foot brushed against hers under the table.

His nickname for her was spoken like a caress. How could she be just friends with this man when her heart wanted so much more?

She was glad when Bella and Dani walked into the room.

"Hey. My Dad wants me to pick up something and bring it home for him so I've got to go. Elle, are you coming with me or with Adam?" Bella looked from her to Adam.

"She's coming with me." Adam's tone was confident and determined.

"Go on home, Bella. I'll go with Adam." For a moment Elle thought of disagreeing with Adam but it was time they talked.

Bella waved at them and walked out.

"Dani and I have plans too. Nice talking with you two." Bree stood to her feet and with a quick wave, left the room.

Suddenly, they were alone. Just the two of them.

Elle fidgeted with a napkin on the table before peering up at Adam. "So, how was your day?"

"Not so great. I kept thinking what a jerk I was last night." Adam's quiet tone unnerved her. A furrow formed on his forehead, his blue eyes solemn and intense. "Sorry for being angry with you. You don't deserve that."

She just sat there for a moment, silent. Adam's piercing gaze was unsettling, but he needed to know where she was coming from.

"Just so we're clear, I want you to know I'm not the kind of girl who would encourage one man while already married to another." The words rushed out of her mouth in an effort to get much of the unpleasant parts of this conversation out of the way as fast as possible.

"I realize that. My irrational fears got the better of me and I'm truly sorry. It won't happen again." Adam's gaze rested on her, and he reached for her hand, toying with her ring.

"Thanks for that. And I'm sorry too, for any part I played in making things more difficult between us." Elle forced a smile, still feeling unsettled.

It surprised her that he admitted to having irrational fears when it came to her. Perhaps Bella was right, and Adam did have some feelings for her.

Yet, her stepmother's words about finally getting rid of past mistakes continued to circle around in her head. She didn't want to be another mistake Adam regretted about his past. It would be best to settle this now, no matter how hard it was.

"I've been thinking about us and the marriage bargain we made." Elle twisted the napkin, her hands only acting out what she was feeling inside. "Maybe we need to go back to the original plan."

"What do you mean?"

"Well, our original agreement was that we would help each other get what we wanted, and then we'd stick to being friends. No messy emotions confusing things, remember?" A knot formed in her belly as she waited his reply.

"That's how we started, yes. We've already gone past that in the last few weeks, don't you think?" His brows knitted in a frown.

"We have, but that's why we've had more arguments lately. It would be better if we didn't let emotions cloud things and just focused on getting through the next ten months as friends." She glanced up at her fake husband only to see his eyes shutter over.

"If that's what you want."

"I do. This will be better for both of us, you'll see. No messy emotions between us to make things get ugly. It'll be easier when it comes time to part ways at the end of this year." For the first time in these weeks, Elle couldn't read what he was thinking and it scared her. It was like a thick wall had suddenly formed between them.

Adam's eyes glazed over, his jaw clinched tight as he looked at her a moment longer.

Inhaling a deep breath, he blew it out slowly and nodded.

He stood abruptly, his posture rigid, and walked with her to the waiting car. The tension in the air was palpable on the drive home.

How she was going to make it through the days and weeks ahead, loving him as she did?

She hadn't realized the deep chasm her new resolve would bring to their relationship.

How would she make it through the next day when she met Adam's mother for lunch?

Somehow she still needed to convince Eliza Stevenson that all was well, and that her son and his new wife were still very much in love.

dam

"IT'S BEEN a pleasure doing business with you, Bobby." Adam stood up and shook the man's outstretched hand.

"And you, Adam. I have a good feeling about our new agreement. Your software is exactly what my connections need." The Houston business tycoon stood straight and smoothed his tie.

"That's what I like to hear. Let's keep in touch." Adam walked Bobby to the door.

Adam ran a hand through his hair as he paced his office.

He should be happier. He should be elated by the fact he'd just signed a million-dollar deal.

Yet, all he could think about was his wife.

He'd hardly slept last night, thinking about their

conversation. She wanted to remain only friends, but how could he do that when she'd become the most important part of his life?

Ever since he married Elle, he'd been in a constant state of emotional turmoil.

Yes, she frustrated him, but he couldn't get enough of her. He longed to be near her, to share their days with each other, to wake up with his wife by his side.

He really didn't like the emotional upheaval.

Normally, he was a guy with a cool head and the calmest man around. He was dedicated to his work and did what he could to avoid messy feelings.

Since he married Elle, his emotions had gone from exasperation to anger then to liking his wife far too much.

Elle made him a little crazy. Sometimes, he wanted to kiss her and sometimes he just wanted to talk some sense into her.

Yet, his home had never been more alive since Elle became part of it.

So, when Elle announced they should go back to being just friends with no messy emotions involved, he knew that's not what he wanted.

He was falling for his new wife, only she had the last laugh when she decided she only wanted to be friends.

Walking over to his desk, he pressed the intercom button to Jack's office.

"Do you have time to talk?"

"I'll be right over."

Adam went to his compact fridge and pulled out two water bottles just as Jack walked through his office door.

"Trouble with work or your love life?"

"More like there's trouble with my non-existent love-life."

"Uh oh. Let's hear it." Jack caught the water bottle Adam threw his way and opened it taking a long drink. Adam paced while Jack stretched out in one of the leather couches.

"I just don't understand. We were getting closer and suddenly she wants to go back to the non-relationship we started with."

"You had a big argument?"

"Yes. Elle was talking to Bobby at the business dinner. But when I saw them together, I wanted to pound a hole in his face." Adam rubbed the back of his neck. "I don't do things like that."

Jack shook his head. "No, not even with Alicia."

"And then Elle tells me she wants to go back to what we agreed to – friendship without all the messy emotions."

"And you don't want that?"

It was time Adam was honest with himself.

"No."

Jack nodded. "She sounds like a skittish racehorse that has been abused by her handler one too many times." As usual Jack had keen insight into the situation. "Take it slow and be gentle and patient with her. She'll come around."

"You're right." Adam nodded.

"And when the time is right, tell her you love her."

Adam turned toward Jack in surprise. "I didn't say anything about love."

"Don't look so shocked. It's as plain as the nose on

your face." Jack finished drinking the rest of his water. "Now, you've just got to tell her."

"You make it sound so simple. It's really tough to lay your heart on the line. There's always that possibility it'll get trampled." Adam collapsed into his office chair in a stupor as he thought about Jack's words.

"True. But, that's why you need to ask yourself if you can live without her. When you know the answer to that, you can chase after what you really want."

"Jack, you might look like a pirate, but you're surprisingly good at understanding people."

"What can I say? It's a gift." Jack grinned and stood to his feet. "Rooting for you, brother."

Adam chuckled as Jack walked out of his office.

Now, all he needed to do was to take Jack's advice. That was easier said than done when it came to his wife.

He'd talk to Elle tonight.

Mentally he rehearsed everything he wanted to say to her. There was so much he longed to tell her.

To start with, he wanted to tell Elle that loving her had changed his life. Since he'd met her, he felt more alive than he'd ever been.

He loved her. Yet, simply telling her that he loved her seemed far too inadequate, especially since there was so much more to how he felt then three simple words could express.

Somehow he needed to get the words out and let his wife know how much she meant to him, even if she insisted that they weren't to talk about messy emotions.

❧

ELLE BRUSHED through her hair and put it up in her usual French twist.

She wanted to be on time for the late afternoon tea with Adam's mom.

She had just got back from another horse therapy training with the children at her father's ranch.

It was really difficult to go there now, as the large for sale sign taunted her, reminding her that she had failed to keep the ranch. She desperately wished there was another way to save her father's ranch, but right now she couldn't see how.

Elle changed quickly into a princess tea-length blue summer dress made of light chiffon. She kept her hair down and slipped her feet into matching blue shoes.

Today she really looked forward to getting to know Eliza better. It just felt a little awkward to talk with her husband's mother, when she was feeling a little annoyed with Adam.

Maybe this would help get her mind off of her own problems.

Elle wrote a quick note to remind Adam of where she was and drove to the city to meet Eliza.

As soon as she stepped into the restaurant, her jaw dropped slightly as she looked up at the glittering chandeliers that hung from the high ceilings.

The front desk and door entrances were lined with mahogany wood and heightened her awareness of the elegant high tea restaurant she entered.

Soon she was led toward Eliza's table. Elle glanced at many women with their daughters who had dressed up in posh dresses, gloves and hats for their high tea experience.

Eliza was dressed in a tea-length blue dress that complimented her eyes.

"Hello Elle." Eliza stood up from her table and kissed her on the cheek.

"Hi, Mom." Today especially, it felt strange to call Eliza that, because of the awkwardness between her and Adam. A new wariness rose up within her.

She longed for the love of a mother, someone just like Eliza. Yet, Elle's marriage to her son was on borrowed time. Any close relationship with Adam's mother was just asking for more pain and heartache.

"This is a beautiful restaurant. Thanks for inviting me to tea."

"I'm glad you like it. It's good to be pampered once in awhile." Eliza winked at her and sighed. "This is so relaxing."

"It is." Elle took a sip of water.

The waiter came and took their order.

"I want to hear all about you." Her mother-in-law sipped her water and peered over at her. "How it's going with your new horse?"

"Really good. I was able to run him most days this week, and he made really good time. It won't be long before he's ready to race." Elle grinned as she remembered that great ride.

"Good." Eliza spoke softly. "I remember when Adam spoke to me about ideas for your birthday gift. I'm so happy he found something you really love."

"Justice is the best gift I've ever had. I'm still surprised by Adam's generous gift."

"That doesn't surprise me at all. Ever since he was a

little boy, Adam always did what he could to make the people he loved happy." Eliza paused for a moment, her gaze focused on Elle. "Whenever I talk to him lately, he speaks highly of you. I can tell you're very special to him."

Elle wanted to believe that was true, but she knew better. This was a marriage based on convenience, not love. Adam made that plain from the beginning.

Still she found herself drawn into the cozy picture Eliza painted of a couple who loved each other.

Adam's mom smiled and toyed with her napkin. "I had a gut feeling — long before Adam's father or even his great-grandfather realized it — that Adam would find a way to come back to the ranch and the horses."

"Daniel was sure Adam would only focus on developing computer software since that was his interest growing up. But I saw how Adam came alive whenever he would visit his great-grandfather's ranch."

"Adam does love Grand's ranch. He's also the most generous and protective man I've ever known." It was true. Elle had experienced it herself.

"He always was, even from a young age." Eliza explained. "He was always taking care of some sort of stray animal whenever he'd go to the ranch. He would help his great-grandfather with the horses, and they would often race together. Adam has always been good with people, often seeing details that others miss."

Eliza turned to Elle, her blue eyes glowing with love for her son as she continued. "I remember one summer when Adam was twelve, his best friend — a neighbor who lived near his great-grandfather's ranch — got hurt in a horse racing accident."

"Joe was hightailing it down a dirt road when the horse shied from some sort of noise, and he went flying through the air. His best friend was paralyzed from the waist down from that accident."

"I'm so sorry."

"It was hard on Adam. It was a difficult time in his life."

"What happened to his friend and the horse?"

"Adam ended up going to Joe's family home to see his friend. When he realized they wanted to get rid of that horse, Adam offered to take the mare to his great grandfather's ranch. It meant so much to Joe, that the horse he loved was taken care of. The horse had cuts all over her body and skittish, too afraid to let anyone near her."

Eliza went on. "But Adam kept feeding, brushing and caring for that mare until she was well again." She smiled and shook her head.

"You should have seen that horse. That mare was the one horse on his great-grandfather's ranch that tested Adam the most. She wouldn't let anyone near her."

Elle's smile weakened. A knot formed in her stomach. Not unlike the horse, she was an orphan and needed someone to help her.

The puzzle pieces began to come together in her mind of all that Adam had done for her ever since she was a child.

He had helped her with her homework from school as a young girl. He had protected her from wild animals like a snake and a bear. And he had protected her from one of the mean farmhands. Later her father fired that man.

Adam was a very protective man — he was a rescuer — he always had been.

Perhaps he'd seen it as his duty to marry and rescue her from her stepmother and to save the ranch from foreclosure?

"Did Adam keep the horse?" The knot grew bigger in Elle's stomach, afraid to hear the answer.

Eliza nodded. "Yes. Adam named that horse Cowgirl. He worked with her, patiently trying to train her and to make the horse feel safe."

Cowgirl was the same horse Adam rode to race against Elle on Big Red when she was a young girl.

"Didn't Adam get tired of Cowgirl's surly moods and then lose interest in that horse after a while?"

"As Adam became a teenager, he began to spend more time with his friends. Cowgirl was still at his great-grandfather's ranch. Whenever Adam could get out to the ranch, he'd ride that horse, spending as much time with her as he could."

"Of course when Adam worked for your father, he saw that horse most of the time. You must remember that."

"I do remember." Elle sighed as memories of spending time with Adam in her childhood, swept over her.

Her mother-in-law continued telling her story. "Later on, when Adam started college, Cowgirl died. Adam was real sad about it for the longest time. But he eventually moved on from that loss, but it was hard on him."

A chilling sensation made its way down Elle's arms, settling in her stomach. She struggled to hide her heartache from her mother-in-law.

All Adam's talk about her being the best thing that had happened to him wasn't the truth.

It was just Adam's way of making Elle feel better about

herself. The truth was he hadn't accepted her as she was, not really.

To him, Elle was a poor orphan girl — the lonely little neighbor girl — who was helpless and in need of being rescued.

Adam didn't believe that she was the best thing that happened to him. And like his friend's horse, Adam would eventually replace her too.

Elle was convinced that his interest in her would wander. She was sure that his feelings for her would wane. Perhaps, they already had.

A numbness spread to Elle's arms and continued down her legs. She felt dead inside — all her hopes for anything more between her and Adam had now been lost.

Somehow, she made it through the rest of the tea with Eliza. She answered her questions and spoke in her usual casual way, hoping that her mother-in-law was none the wiser to how she really felt.

Meanwhile, for Elle it felt like the whole world had suddenly crashed down around her.

By the time she drove home the sun had set. It was pouring rain as she arrived back at the ranch.

She felt sick to her stomach as she got out of the car.

Her heart galloped as she saw Adam's car and walked up the front steps.

What would she say to him?

Uncertain, she opened the door to the house.

Her husband stood there like he'd been waiting for her. The top two buttons of his white shirt were unbuttoned and it looked like he'd been running his hand through his hair all day.

"Hey." Adam's gaze followed her as she hung up her jacket and set her purse down on the counter.

"Hi. Do you want something to drink?" Elle murmured as she walked to the table and set her things down.

Adam followed her, leaning against the doorway.

Her hands shook slightly as she grabbed a couple of glasses from the cupboard. She didn't turn around as she spoke. "How was your day?"

"Not so great." Adam's quiet tone made Elle turn around. She saw a furrow form on his forehead, his blue eyes solemn and intense. "How was yours?"

"Good." She just stood there for a moment, silent. Adam's piercing gaze made her nervous.

Elle forced a smile at Adam, feeling unsettled.

"Did you have a good time with my mother? I hope high tea was type of pampering you hoped for, Cowgirl."

Elle recoiled at the nickname. "Why do you call me that?"

"Cowgirl?"

She gave a sharp nod, before adding ice to each glass.

"I'm not really sure." Adam rubbed a hand along his jaw. "I did have a horse with that name once."

"The one you brought back to your great-grandfather's ranch after your friend's accident?" She glanced at him once before turning her back to him to pour water into each cup.

He peered over at her, curiosity etched on his face. "Yes, that's the one. How did you know?"

"Your mom said something about it today." Her throat tightened and she tried swallowing away the bitter taste that had formed in her mouth. She turned around to face him. "Your mom told me that horse was a piece of work."

Adam chuckled at the memory. "It took a little bit of patience, but the mare eventually came around."

"Sort of like I did." Elle's voice wavered, still unable to turn around to face him.

"You? How do you mean?" Adam glanced up, surprised. "I thought we were talking about my old horse, cowgirl."

"That is what we're talking about." Elle twisted around to look him in the eye, steadying herself on the counter behind her. "As I think about it, there's seems to be similar traits between your old horse and me. *I'm* much like Cowgirl."

Adam looked startled. "That's... well that's the silliest thing I've ever heard."

"Maybe. But, I really want to ask you why you would marry a girl like me — a woman who was desperate for money to save her Dad's ranch? You could've married someone else and not given away that much money."

"Well, it's like I told you before, all the other women were superficial. You were at least honest and real about what you needed."

"And you wanted to save me from losing the ranch." Elle choked out the words, as now that part wasn't true anymore.

Her stepmother's plan to sell the ranch, meant she was going to lose the land anyway.

"Well... I suppose that's true." Adam stuttered a little, and spoke quieter as if trying to calm her down. "But I wanted to have you nearby as a neighbor too, so making sure you had enough money to pay off the mortgage and keep your late father's land seemed like the ideal solution to both our problems."

"I still think it was a lot of money to give away. Especially, when there must be many women who would've married you for nothing." Elle continued.

"I didn't care that it was a lot of money. I wanted to do something that would be helpful."

"This may come as a shock to you Adam Stevenson, but I do care. Just because I'm poor and not like the upperclass women you're used to dating, doesn't mean that I need someone to feel sorry for me." Elle wrapped her arms around herself and glared at her husband.

"I didn't do it because I felt sorry for you!"

Elle dropped her hands to her sides and balled them into a fist. "What I think, is that out of all the women you knew I needed to be saved the most. You certainly didn't marry me because I was someone that was in your social class, like Alicia Wentworth. And you certainly didn't marry me because I came from the right family."

Adam sighed and waited a moment before he spoke again. "I think it would be better if we gave each other some space — and time to calm down."

"I don't want time to calm down!" She choked out the words in desperation.

To her dismay, her voice cracked.

Adam stepped forward and reached for her. "Listen, cowgirl..."

"Don't call me that!" Elle stepped back and away from his reach. Taking a deep breath she went on, "I want to know the truth Adam. Ever since we began this fake marriage, have I been someone you felt sorry for and felt you needed to save?"

"Well the truth is, you did need me." Adam soft words pinged her heart with their truth. "You needed the money to save your father's ranch. In some ways you were like that broken horse I saved years ago."

"So, that's the reason you did it." She breathed out slowly, her legs wobbling a little. She steadied herself by putting a hand against the wall.

"Yes. But, the reason soon changed for me." Adam repeated his words as if trying to make her understand. "You were so scared of losing your Dad's ranch and it seemed like there was hardly anyone around to help you."

Elle remembered how desperate she had been to do something — anything to save her late father's ranch. She wanted to get out from under her stepmother's demanding ways and to save his ranch — the land she loved so much.

But now it seemed that all her hopes and dreams were lost.

"You're right. I needed you to rescue me in the beginning." A steely quality entered Elle's voice and she stood in front of her husband her posture rigid and resolute. "But, I never wanted to be someone that you pitied."

Deep lines formed on his forehead, his blue eyes intense and he shook his head. He opened his mouth to speak but Elle interrupted before he could begin.

"I'm going to the barn to see the horses. I need some space to think." Elle grabbed a jacket and slipped on her boots. Turning as she got to the door she spoke firmly. "Don't follow me."

"Elle, wait..." Adam called after her but she kept running toward the barn.

The pouring rain had soaked through her jacket and pants by the time she reached the barn.

She hurried to Justice's stall.

Hearing his soft whinny, she patted his neck and hugged him. She stood there a moment, her mind flooded with chaos, confusion and hurt.

Suddenly it wasn't enough to just be close to the horse she loved so much, she needed to feel his power and strength beneath her. Before long she had his bridle on and slid onto his back.

Heavy rain sliced through the air, pelting her like a thousand little needles, as she rode her horse out of the barn. Even the lights that surrounded the outskirts of the racetrack, were barely noticeable through the torrent of rain.

All Elle could think of as Justice trotted toward the racetrack was that she'd lost everything she ever wanted.

Tears fell down her cheeks, mixing unheeded with the downpour.

First, she'd lost her parents who both died leaving her alone. Then her stepmother decided to sell her Dad's land and now she was going to lose the ranch she loved so much.

But, the last loss was the most devastating.

Losing Adam.

He might have rescued her with a marriage pact, but she had grown to love him.

Now she realized her love had blinded her to the truth. She was someone for Adam to feel sorry for, in the same way that broken horse had been all those years ago.

Her husband might even believe that he had started to feel something more for her now, but time would prove him wrong.

Her stepmother's words went round and round in her head once again. *I'm guessing Adam has already figured out what a poor choice he made for a wife and regrets that decision.*

Adam's mother said he lost interest in that broken horse he rescued years ago and shifted his interests to his friends. She was convinced the same thing would happen to her.

There was no guarantee that things would be different with her, that within a few short weeks or months he wouldn't regret that he married her.

Elle urged Justice into a run when they got to the race-track. He went slower than usual, the heavy mud clinging like paste to his legs.

Without warning, her horse spooked and jerked to one side.

Shocked at the sudden movement, Elle tried desperately to stay on the horse, but felt herself falling through the air.

Her last thought was that her father had also died in the rain…

CHAPTER FOURTEEN

dam

ADAM PACED BACK and forth in front of the kitchen window.

Not ten minutes ago, he had watched Elle walk inside the barn. She still hadn't returned.

Knots of anxiety formed in his belly.

He was still processing everything his wife said.

How could she believe he felt sorry for her when she was everything he'd ever wanted in a woman?

Yes, he admitted that he wanted to help Elle save her father's ranch when he married her. But she also helped him so that he could inherit his great grandfather's ranch.

To his way of thinking, they had helped each other.

What was going on in that wonderful, but anxious mind of hers that would make her think he pitied her?

Elle may have wanted some time alone but seeing her so upset tonight made him worry.

He couldn't wait any longer.

Pulling on his jacket and boots, he decided it was time to find her and finish their conversation.

He hurried out the door, the heavy rain made it hard to see. The yard light by the barn flickered, and he could barely see it through the downpour.

Pulling the hood of his jacket over his head, he trudged through the mud.

Opening the barn door, he stopped suddenly.

The pounding of horse hooves in the distance caught his attention.

Pivoting, Adam ran toward the yard lights that surrounded the racetrack.

As he dashed around the corner, he caught sight of Justice running around the racetrack. There was no rider on his back.

The racehorse ran fast, seemingly without any injuries. But where was Elle?

Worried, Adam sprinted onward to get a better view of the track. His heart knotted in his chest as he ran.

Suddenly he saw her. His wife lay broken and twisted in the mud.

His heart flipped upwards, punching at the base of his throat.

Adam rushed toward her, panic flooding him. What if she was badly hurt or worse? He should have stopped her.

He should have done everything in his power to keep her safe. Yet he'd let her go out into the pouring rain. If she was hurt, he would never forgive himself.

Finally he reached her side.

"Elle. Sweetheart, talk to me." Adam knelt by her side, his hand touching her face. She lay motionless, not responding to his touch. Her eyes were closed with not so much as a flicker as he spoke her name.

He placed a finger along her neck desperate to find a pulse, breathing a sigh of relief when he found a faint heart beat.

Pulling out his phone Adam dialed nine-one-one. They told him not to move her but to stay with her, and they would be there quickly.

He called Jed, asking him to find Elle's horse and bring him home safely.

By the time Adam had finished calling his family to let them know what happened, the ambulance drove up. The EMT's gently put her on a stretcher and into the ambulance.

Adam's hands and legs trembled as he sat beside her and held Elle's hand, whispering all the things he wanted to say, praying he got the chance to say them.

After a brief examination, a nurse walked up to him, "We're taking your wife down for a MRI. The doctor will be out in awhile to let you know how she's doing."

"Thank you." Adam sat in the waiting room,

Fear gripped him as he thought of what the doctor would find. He worried about the seriousness of her condition.

"Hey." Jack walked into the waiting room, with Adam's mother at his side. Eliza hugged her son before asking, "How is she?"

"The doctor's doing tests, but she is still unconscious.

She was just lying there so still and pale. I'm real worried." Adam rubbed the back of his neck as he paced a short path in the waiting room.

"I'm so sorry, son. We're here for you. Whatever you need." His mother held his hand, a comforting gesture.

"I know, and I'm grateful. Thanks for coming."

"You know we wouldn't be anywhere else. Our family sticks together through thick and thin." Jack clapped him on the back before finding a comfortable chair to sit in.

"Thanks, Jack." Adam sat beside them fidgeting, until finally the doctor walked through the door.

"Adam Stevenson?"

"Yes." Adam stood up, his legs unsteady.

"I have the test results from your wife's scan." The doctor's face revealed nothing as he delivered the news. "We've determined she has mild head trauma, cracked ribs and a fractured arm."

"The last two will heal in a few weeks, but a head trauma can be unpredictable. You can visit her quietly but, don't expect her to respond to you." The doctor studied him for a moment before he continued, "You say she was riding her race horse?"

"Yes."

"Then, I'd have to say your wife is one lucky lady. Her injuries could have been much worse. She's lucky to be alive. " As the doctor walked away, for the first time Adam realized how close he'd come to losing Elle.

"I need to see her." Adam turned, speaking quickly to his mom and Jack.

"Go. We'll be here when you get back."

Adam found a nurse who led him to his wife's room.

His legs went weak at the sight of her still form lying on the bed.

Elle was so pale and lifeless, so unlike the energetic and feisty woman he knew and loved.

As he sat beside the bed, he wrapped both hands around her cold one.

"I'm so sorry. I never meant for this to happen." He kissed the top of her hand. "I should have stopped you from running outside in the rain. I knew how upset you were and should have gone after you. It's my fault that you're lying here broken."

Tears welled up in Adam's eyes and he whispered. "Please, talk to me sweetheart. I need you in all your feisty and sometimes stubborn ways to come back to me. Nothing is the same without you."

Adam whispered to her, and she just lay on the bed, unblinking and motionless. The only sound was the steady beat of the heart monitor.

Memories spun around in his head. Working with Elle at her Dad's ranch and how she made him do most of the grunge work, made him smile. Even though he didn't like mucking out stalls, he liked it that she had a lot of spunk.

That she agreed to this fake marriage was nothing short of a surprise to him — she looked beautiful on their wedding day.

He had surprised her with the honeymoon trip of the Royal Ascot horserace, knowing she'd appreciate it. But, Elle was the one who surprised him with her excitement for life. She had made him come alive. Giving her that race horse had been a fun surprise, her tears of happiness making it worth every penny.

There were so many good memories with Elle. And her compassion for Bree and others neared the top of his list. She did so much for others around her. She was one of those people who gave, not expecting anything in return.

He'd become jaded from the women he had dated and some of his other connections. It made him really grateful for who Elle was. She was real and honest about who she was and what she wanted.

Her compassion and generous spirit made him want to be a better man. He wanted to be a better husband, and wanted to make their marriage real and lasting.

The door to the hospital room opened and Bella walked toward Elle's bedside. A sliver of the morning sunlight slipped through the blinds in the hospital window.

"I came as soon as I could." Bella sat on the other side of the bed. "She's so pale and still."

"Yes, the doctor doesn't know how long it will be before she wakes up. So we just wait."

Bella held her best friend's other hand between hers. "Come on, Elle. Come back to us."

They sat in silence for a few minutes.

"You say she went riding in the rain and fell off Justice?" Bella asked.

"Yes."

"That's so unlike Elle. She must not have been thinking straight."Bella knew her best friend well.

"We had an argument. Elle told me she was going to visit the horses and that I wasn't to follow her." Adam stood and paced. "But I should have gone after her. It's my fault she's lying here hurt."

"You didn't know she would decide to ride. It's not your fault." Bella turned to him. "She must be more upset about her stepmother selling her father's ranch than I realized."

"What?" Adam spun around, facing Bella. "I didn't know that. From the beginning, that's all she ever wanted was her Dad's ranch."

He stopped and slipped on his jacket.

"I need to go. Will you text or call me if she wakes up?" Adam put his jacket on and slipped his phone in his pocket.

"Yes, of course." Bella looked at him as if he'd taken leave of his senses.

"I'll be back as soon as I can."

Adam hurried out of the hospital determined to do what he could to make things right for Elle.

IT WASN'T until late evening that Adam arrived back at the hospital.

He was tired, but satisfied.

His mom and Jack had gone home, but Bella still sat by Elle's side.

Seeing Adam, she got up. "She hasn't woken up yet, but I'm confident she will soon. I'm headed home for some rest. Text me if she wakes up, okay?"

Adam nodded, glancing quickly at Bella before turning back to his wife.

He sat by her bedside once again. After watching his wife and seeing no movement, he decided to take a short nap. When he woke up, a few rays of sunrise drifted in through the window.

Adam sat up, stretched, and looked at Elle. He reached for her hand and held it for the longest time, just staring at her.

Suddenly it was like a dam burst inside him.

"Elle sweetheart, please come back to me." He whispered, his grip tightening on her hand. "You need to come back from wherever you are. Bella needs you. Joanna needs you. I need you."

A tear ran down his cheek as he stared at his wife. Her once laughing face now pale and unmoving. "You might not believe it, but you are the best thing that's ever happened to me. The last thing I feel for you is charity or pity. You are beautiful to me just as you are. I love your smile. I love your laugh. I even love your sass. I finally realize how much I love you. Just when it's too late."

Adam took a deep breath and wiped the tears that flowed unheeded down his cheeks.

"I love you." A low moan filled the room, and his voice cracked. "But Elle, I'm no good for you. You know why? You nearly died riding that racehorse. I would never have given that animal to you if I would've known it would hurt you."

His voice was husky and raw. "The worst part is that I couldn't protect you. The truth is, all the people I love end up dying. First, my dad died from a heart attack. Maybe if he wouldn't have had so much stress, he wouldn't have died so young. I should've done something to help to relieve some of his anxiety. Then your father died in that accident."

"Elle, you've got to understand that I tried to stop your dad from going out in the rain that night. I told him we should stay at the hotel because the weather report said it was freezing rain and the roads were already turning to ice. But, for some reason, it didn't stop your father from driving that night. He said he'd be careful but he needed to get home to his girls." Adam's voice grew hoarse and he gripped her hand like it was his lifeline.

"I followed him, hoping to sort of keep watch over him, but it was too late. His truck swerved off that icy road and into that ravine. I ran down the hill to see if I could help him, but he lay there bleeding and broken. His last words to me were *tell Elle I'm sorry and I love her.*"

A gentle squeeze on his hand caused him to look up. "That's what you came to tell me at my father's funeral." Elle's voice sound raspy. "I didn't realize you tried to stop my father from driving that night. I'm so sorry I was angry with you for so long. Will you forgive me?"

Adam's heart shuddered away in his ears at the sound of her voice. He expelled a long sigh of relief and for a long moment just stared at her.

"Yes. All that matters now, is that you're okay." Adam embraced her, his arms gentle like she was made of glass.

"Did you mean it when you said you loved me?" Her eyes widened as they searched his.

"Yes." Adam leaned over her, taking in the sweep of her eyelashes and the curve of her mouth.

He bent his head to kiss her, just touching his lips to hers, when a nurse opened the door to check on her patient. Finding Elle awake, she pressed the button and called for the doctor.

The next hour was busy with the doctors checking on Elle. By the time they'd finished, Bella had arrived, wanting to talk with her best friend.

"I'll leave the two of you to talk." Adam kissed Elle on the cheek and whispered, "This is for you."

He placed an envelope in her hand and squeezing her hand gently, he walked out of his wife's hospital room.

As he drove back to the ranch, Adam couldn't stop thinking about Elle. He loved her. But he'd almost lost her.

She had almost died because of him.

Throughout his life, those that he loved, he couldn't protect. People he loved and who loved him ending up dying.

Adam couldn't do that to Elle. He wouldn't do that to the woman he'd come to adore.

He needed to be strong.

He needed to remind himself that Elle was better off — safer — without him in her life.

He loved his wife enough to let her go.

AFTER FIVE DAYS in the hospital, Elle was released to go home. Her ribs hurt and her arm was in a cast, but she was alive.

Bella picked her up and drove her back to the ranch. Elle wondered why she hadn't seen Adam since he handed her the envelope and left the hospital.

Adam hadn't returned to the hospital, even though his mom and brother had stopped by almost everyday.

When she'd asked Jack why Adam didn't visit, he told her there'd been a bit of a crisis with the software and the management team. Adam had been working long hours and barely sleeping trying to fix things.

Elle had just nodded, but she was worried about him.

Something about his actions and words didn't add up.

Memories of what Adam had told her as she lay in the hospital went round and round in her head.

He loved her.

But, he thought he wasn't any good for her. He believed because he couldn't protect the people he loved, they were better off without him.

When Adam handed her the envelope that day, she didn't realize how it would change her life.

He had given her the title deed to her father's ranch. He had given her a new freedom. He had given back her dream.

It was too much. She didn't feel right about accepting it.

As she got out of the car, she knew what she needed to do.

"You okay?" Bella walked toward her and hugged her close.

"Yes. I feel good." It felt like a breath of fresh air being home at last.

"I'll leave you then. But, call me if you need anything, right?" Bella turned just before she got to her truck and her eyes pointed, waiting for her reply.

"I will. I promise." Elle laughed at Bella's tendency to mother her.

After Bella left, Elle walked toward the barn and horse pasture. She was about to do one of the hardest things she'd ever done, but it needed to be done.

She dialed the number of a horse owner she had met who loved horse racing. After she had come to an agreement with him, she went to rest her arms on the fence to watch Justice as he roamed and romped in the pasture.

It was a pleasure to look at him. She desperately wanted to ride him, but she needed to wait three months before getting back on a horse.

After awhile, a truck and trailer drove onto the yard.

Just as Elle walked over to meet him, Adam's car drove onto the yard. Her husband got out and walked toward her.

"Hi Elle." Adam stood close to her, his hands in his pockets. Seeing the older man get out of his vehicle he asked, "What is Mr. Crenshaw doing here?"

"I called him. I've decided to sell Justice." Unbidden, tears filled her eyes. She hastily wiped them away.

"Why would you do that? You love that horse." Adam put a gentle hand under her chin, his eyes searching hers.

"Well, you don't feel like I'm safe riding Justice, especially since the accident. I want you to know that Justice or any other horse is not as important to me as you are. It just seemed like this was the only way I could show you that." Tears streamed down her cheeks as she looked up at Adam. "I love you more than anything, Adam. I really do."

Taking a step toward her, Adam pulled her close into a tight embrace.

"Ah, Elle. I love you too, sweetheart. I tried to stay away from you, but I just couldn't." He breathed a ragged breath and pulled back so he could look at her.

"I'm so afraid I won't be able to protect you. You've already suffered because of me." A vein popped in Adam's neck and his voice cracked.

His finger ran the length of the cast on her arm. The despair she saw in his eyes tore at her soul.

"No, that's not true. None of this was your fault. I chose to ride Justice in the rain and I fell off. It's my own fault." Elle went on. "Both of our father's deaths is not your fault either."

"I've blamed myself for so many years, I don't know how to forgive myself and accept that I'm not to blame." He took a pained breath, his haunted holding hers.

"We'll do this together, okay?"

A deep sigh seemed to resonate deep within him before he spoke. "All right, we'll get through this together."

"But I meant it when I said that Justice isn't as important to me as you are, Adam." Elle's eyes shimmered with tears.

"So, if you don't want me to ride anymore, I won't. I will choose to give it up because I love you more than any of those dreams I have for myself." Elle reached up to touch her husband's cheek, pouring her heart into her words. "That's why I'm selling Justice."

"Aww, Elle. I understand and love your self-sacrifice and it means the world to me." He kissed her hand. "But, I don't want you to sell him. I want you to keep the horse you love. And when the doctor says it's okay to ride again, then you should do it." Adam placed his hand over hers.

"Are you sure? Because I was also going to use the money from selling my horse to pay you back for giving me the title deed for my dad's ranch." Elle felt that the gift was too much.

"Sweetheart, I don't want you to pay me back. I gave that deed to you because I love you. Not for any other reason that might be going through that beautiful head of yours."

A man coughed in the background, and Elle stepped away from Adam, heat flooding her cheeks because she'd forgotten about their guest.

They explained about their decision not to sell the horse. He was upset at first, but was appeased when they invited him and his family to Justice's next race.

Looking back at Adam, Elle needed to hear his words again. "You gave the deed to me because you love me?"

"Yes." Adam's tender smile was nearly her undoing. "But if it makes you feel better, why don't you consider the title deed a donation to your horse therapy nonprofit organization?"

"Hmm. Never thought of it that way. But I like your first reason better and I accept your generous gift with overwhelming thanks." She looked up at him, her heart in her eyes.

"I'm glad." Adam's eyes took on a seriousness. "But, I'd prefer, if you didn't live on your Dad's ranch. I was rather hoping we could switch the terms of our marriage pact."

"What do you mean?" She pinched her eyebrows together in confusion until he got down on one knee in front of her.

"Elle Jennings Stevenson, I love you with all my heart.

Will you do me the honor of marrying me again, this time to become my real wife?" As Adam's blue eyes looked up at her, she noticed a new calmness there, instead of that haunted look that had surrounded him.

"Yes, Adam I will." She placed her hands on both sides of his face and locked her eyes with his, as her love for him nearly overwhelmed her.

He stood to his feet and gently placed his hands on her waist, pulling her close.

Stepping back, he put his hands on both sides of her face and leaning down Adam placed his lips on hers.

Elle savored the sweetness of his kiss. This wonderful man who at first inspired her to anger, now inspired her to love so deeply.

Adam wrapped his arms around her. Elle met his kiss with so many wonderful emotions rising up on the inside of her.

She now looked forward to the future. With Adam at her side, she could do anything. She could hope and dream, knowing he would be there for her.

Elle made a commitment in that moment, that somehow Adam would have the confidence of knowing his wife would always be by his side too.

CHAPTER FIFTEEN

hree months later…

ADAM SQUISHED the sand between his toes and watched as the evening sun skittered across the lake.

The violin quartet he hired played soft music in the background as he waited for his bride.

Ever since he had proposed to Elle for the second time, she had been excited about planning a vow renewal ceremony.

At first, he'd been unsure about it, but he wanted to do whatever it took to make his wife happy. When he agreed, the joy on her face had made it all worth it.

The setting for their vow renewal was perfect. With Grand's ranch house in the background, Adam was over-whelmed with a sense of belonging and unwavering love.

This simple ceremony on the beach, surrounded by a few family and friends, was just right.

Elle had invited her students from the horse therapy programs. They all showed up with their caregivers. Bree and Dani sat near the back of the row of chairs, Joanna next to them.

A couple of his friends also came to his wedding, along with a few of Elle's friends from their small town. Adam was thankful for their support.

His mom, grandmom and brothers all stood near him, smiles on their faces. Jack stood by his side as best man.

Adam couldn't help but grin at Jack whose eyes were riveted on the maid of honor that walked toward them.

Bella looked beautiful in a simple yellow summer dress. Her long dark brown hair hung down her back in waves and the tiny splash of baby's breath by her right ear, only added to her beauty.

Adam looked forward to teasing Jack later.

At this moment however, he was anxiously awaiting the first glimpse of his bride.

Then he saw her.

Elle stepped out from behind the row of trees that separated the ranch land from the beach.

Her hand rested on top of his granddad's arm, as she walked toward Adam with a beautiful smile that lit up her face.

His bride was dressed in a tea-length white summer dress with long blond hair that hung loose to her waist.

She held yellow, white and red roses that were scattered with baby's breath. A single red rose was pinned in her hair with baby's breath adding a delicate earthy touch.

She was beautiful.

Seeing her walk gracefully toward him now, a smile on her lips, felt like he was looking at a little bit of heaven on earth.

Looking at her now, nobody would be able to tell that she'd lain broken and bruised in the hospital only three months ago. The cast was off her arm and the concussion and cracked ribs were healing.

He was so thankful that she'd come back to him.

Adam held out his hand as she reached for him, tucking her smaller one inside his.

Leaning over, he whispered in her ear, "You're beautiful."

Elle's cheeks blossomed with pink and only added to her glow of the blushing bride.

The pastor spoke of marriage for a few minutes before he asked them to repeat their vows.

Looking into Elle's beautiful eyes, he poured his heart into the words that would bind them together forever.

"You were ten when I first caught you, sneaking into my grand's horse pasture. When you got on Big Red, I raced you on my horse, Cowgirl. You still won. I realized something. It's your courage, determination and compassion that won me over since that first day I met you."

"Only now, you are a beautiful woman with an even bigger heart. We've shared many memories through the years, some good, some not so good. I'm sad to say, fear held me back from accepting your forgiveness for awhile." Adam swallowed emotions that clogged his throat.

"Your acceptance and love saved me, and I was able to see for the first time the real treasure of who you are. I'm thankful for our memories, and I look forward to making many more new ones in our future together. I love you, Elle."

Elle's green eyes filled with tears and seemed to stare into his soul.

In the beginning, he hadn't wanted a real marriage, but since he fell in love with Elle it seemed he couldn't wait for this moment.

No longer would their marriage be fake. After today, they would have a real marriage based on love and commitment.

Gently, he reached for her. With his arms around her waist, he lowered his head and gently placed his lips on hers.

The sweetness of her kiss intoxicated him. He breathed deeply of her floral scent, loving the way her arms held tightly to him.

Having Elle in his arms, felt like coming home.

ELLE'S KNEES weakened and her pulse quickened as Adam's warm lips pressed against her own.

Her arms slipped further around his waist, holding tightly to her husband. Love had melted her heart and turned her emotions into a gooey, messy puddle.

She loved every second of it.

It had been such a long wait to find a husband who would love her like this. This kind of love had been on her list from the beginning, but she never really thought it would happen for her.

Believing that she wasn't worthy to be loved and that she was someone others pitied had all been lies. Those lies had created wounds and the reason she had put up walls around her heart.

She saw that clearly now.

Her stepmother had tried to convince her that Adam would regret marrying her. That was another lie that she realized wasn't true.

Adam really did love her. He didn't pity or feel sorry for her. He had wanted Elle to keep Justice, and had given her the deed to her dad's ranch because he loved her.

And now Elle truly belonged to a family again. For so long, she had felt lost and displaced, and she'd been convinced that would never change.

Marrying Adam had shifted everything. Now they were a real family and she had been added to the Stevenson family. It was the most wonderful feeling in the world.

Her heart overflowed with contentment.

Adam ended the kiss, his eyes flickering with tenderness.

When he pulled his arms away, Elle sighed missing her husband's warmth.

As they were announced as husband and wife, everyone clapped.

"We've decided to change the rules for our wedding. Instead of everyone giving us gifts, we decided to give each of you a gift. Beneath your chairs you'll find an assortment of gift cards, so you can enjoy a Shopping Spree on us." Adam's unexpected announcement was greeted with loud gasps and cheers from family and friends alike.

Elle had been surprised and excited when Adam mentioned that he wanted to do that earlier that week. Her husband continually amazed her at how generous he was with everyone he knew.

"You've made everyone so happy by doing that."

"We did. From now on it's us together."

"I love that." Elle slipped her hand in his. While their guests were busy looking at their gifts, Adam and Elle walked to where the sand touched the water.

"I was going to surprise you, but I can't wait."

"What is it?"

"I thought we'd fly to the Caribbean Islands with our first stop at St. Lucia for our second honeymoon. I've chartered a yacht that will take us from one island to the next and we can stay as long as we like at each island."

"What a great surprise."

"Well, I need you rested up for when you ride Justice in the race when we get back home." He chuckled, his eyes crinkling with playfulness.

"I'll be plenty ready to ride Justice, don't you worry about that." Elle had looked forward to her doctor saying it was fine for her to ride and just this week he'd said she could try again.

Adam laughed out loud at her eagerness.

"But that's not the end of my surprises." Her husband's eyebrows quirked up. "After that, I thought we'd fly to Hawaii to visit your Aunt."

"Oh Adam, you remembered about my aunt?" Her eyes

glistened with tears and, she reached up to kiss him on the cheek. "You're so thoughtful, thank you."

"Well I've learned how important it is to feel the love of family. You taught me that." He pulled her close and put both arms around her.

They stood there for a long time, looking at the sunset on the lake.

"This is the same spot I saw you months ago." Adam's warm breath whispered against the top of her head.

"I remember. You were so handsome." Elle frowned as memories of that day came back. "And I was so angry and rude to you."

"We've both had fears and misconceptions. I'm grateful we've chosen to love each other instead." Adam moved closer.

Placing his hands on her cheeks, he tipped up her chin. "Our marriage pact was the best thing I ever did because it brought me you. I love you."

A single tear rolled down her cheek at his words.

She would never get tired of hearing him say those three little words.

EPILOGUE

ACK

"WELCOME to the first horse racing event at the newly renovated Walker Stevenson horse racing track." The announcer began as Jack stepped onto the grandstand, and found his brother.

"Hey, Adam. Looks like I got here just in time." Jack playfully punched his brother on the shoulder before he sat down. "By the way, the place looks really good. Grand would be proud of all these new designs and renovations."

"Thanks, I think so too." Adam looked over at him. "I haven't seen you for over a month now. How's it going?"

"Good. Still busy creating new designs and working on the Rose Adventure Park blueprints." In fact, Jack had been busier than ever.

The deadline to complete the designs for the theme park to show the town council, was looming before him.

He was so busy right now, it made him a little jealous of his brother's new tan and the sappy smile on his face. "You look well rested."

"It's amazing what a few weeks with a new bride will do for you. You should try it sometime." From the goofy look on Adam's face, he could tell his brother had it bad.

Adam had definitely fallen in love.

"I'll leave that up to you and our three younger brothers." Jack was happy his brother had found his happily ever after and had settled down. But Jack had already experienced the sting of rejection. He wasn't willing to go there again.

"Hey, forget about her." It always surprised Jack how well his brother knew him. "Just because she couldn't see beyond that scar, doesn't mean there isn't a woman out there who will."

Four years ago, he'd chased after some thugs who had grabbed a teenage girl. Her father was a friend of Jack's, and he had to do something.

He chased the offender down and as he was grabbing the girl, he was rewarded with an ugly cut to his face.

After the stitches came out, his wife Elin saw him for the first time. Memories of her words haunted him still. *I can't see this day after day, Jack. I mean before you looked sort of like a rugged modern-day Tarzan, which I liked. But now, you look awful. You look horrible. You look beastly. I just can't be with you... not now.*

Since that day, he had poured himself into his designs, often asking his brother Gabe or someone he hired to be the front spokesperson so clients wouldn't be terrorized by his scar.

Jack had even gone so far as to buy land in the mountains behind Paradise Lake. He built himself a large log house there, surrounded by trees and mountains just so he could hide away.

"She's forgotten." Jack said, forcing his usual cavalier smile.

Adam's blue eyes narrowed, a groove forming between his eyebrows. Jack knew his brother well and could tell that he wasn't convinced.

"The horses are at the starting gate." Jack sighed in relief at the announcer's words, grateful for the interruption.

"Where's Elle?" Jack stood to his feet along with the rest of the crowd. Good thing Adam always had good seats at the front or it would be difficult to see the race.

"She's riding Justice today." Adam pointed to one of the eight thoroughbreds who were at the starting gate.

Jack stared a little closer. Sure enough, he could see a few strands of Elle's blond hair stick out from the rider in blue.

"I'm nervous for her, but I promised. And I'll just have to trust that she'll be fine." Adam ran his hand through his hair, a nervous habit from when they were kids.

"She will be. Elle's a good rider."

"Yeah." Adam sighed as he watched the agitated horses at the starting gate.

"Man, so this is what it's like to fall hard for a woman." Jack's mouth twitched in amusement at the nervous wreck that was his brother. "I think I'll pass."

"Don't be too quick to downplay the power of love, Jack. You just have to find the right woman." Adam gave his brother a lopsided grin.

"I don't see that happening anytime soon. Besides, I'm not even dating anyone right now."

"You might be surprised at how the right woman simply shows up when it's your turn for love, Jack." His mouth curved into a smile.

Well, his brother might have found the right woman, but it seemed a little more difficult for Jack.

He needed some girl who was a bit of a tomboy and lady all rolled into one.

He needed someone who didn't mind living in the quiet of the mountains at least some of the time.

He also needed someone who wouldn't run away as far and as fast as she could at the sight of his scar.

No, Jack couldn't see himself finding a woman to love anytime soon.

Love simply wasn't possible... not for him.

If you enjoyed reading this book, I'd be deeply grateful if you would consider leaving a review at your favorite digital retail store.

Are you ready to read Jack's Story?
Start Reading The Billionaire's Marriage Contract Today!

Jack's hardened his heart to love.

But, his great-grandfather's will states he must marry in 60 days to receive his inheritance.

Bella's determined to prove her independence to her father.

But, her dad's sudden heart attack forces her to take over his project and finish the design contract with the beastly Jack Stevenson.

Love wasn't part of the plan.

ABOUT THE AUTHOR

Melody Archer lives in Alberta with her husband and their four young adults.

Recently, her oldest son married his wife from Brazil and their family has been enjoying getting to know their new daughter-in-love.

She loves new and classic romantic movies, green smoothies and going on adventures with her family.

Melody would love to connect with you below. :)

facebook.com/memorablefictionbooks

instagram.com/memorablefictionbooks

bookbub.com/profile/melody-archer

pinterest.com/memorablefictionbooks

youtube.com/@memorablefictionbooks

9 781998 833634